*Priv*

New *X Rated* titles from *X Libris*:

| | |
|---|---|
| Game of Masks | Roxanne Morgan |
| Acting It Out | Vanessa Davies |
| Private Act | Zara Devereux |
| Who Dares Sins | Roxanne Morgan |

The *X Libris* series:

| | |
|---|---|
| The Pleasure Principle | Emma Allan |
| Arousing Anna | Nina Sheridan |
| Playing the Game | Selina Seymour |
| Pleasuring Pamela | Nina Sheridan |
| The Women's Club | Vanessa Davies |
| Saturnalia | Zara Devereux |
| Shopping Around | Mariah Greene |
| Velvet Touch | Zara Devereux |
| The Gambler | Tallulah Sharpe |
| Eternal Kiss | Anastasia Dubois |
| Forbidden Desires | Marina Anderson |
| Wild Silk | Zara Devereux |
| Letting Go | Cathy Hunter |
| Two Women | Emma Allan |
| Pleasure Bound | Susan Swann |
| Educating Eleanor | Nina Sheridan |
| Silken Bonds | Zara Devereux |
| Fast Learner | Ginnie Bond |
| Rough Trade | Emma Allan |
| Liberating Lydia | Nina Sheridan |
| Cirque Erotique | Mikki Leone |
| Lessons in Lust | Emma Allan |
| Lottery Lovers | Vanessa Davies |
| Isle of Desire | Zara Devereux |
| Overexposed | Ginnie Bond |
| Black Stockings | Emma Allan |
| Perfect Partners | Natalie Blake |
| Legacy of Desire | Marina Anderson |
| Searching for Sex | Emma Allan |

# Private Parties

## Stephanie Ash

An *X Libris* Book

First published in Great Britain in 2000
by X Libris

Copyright © Stephanie Ash, 2000

The moral right of the author has been asserted.

*All characters in this publication are
fictitious and any resemblance to real
persons, living or dead, is purely coincidental.*

All rights reserved.
No part of this publication may be reproduced,
stored in a retrieval system, or transmitted, in
any form or by any means, without the prior
permission in writing of the publisher, nor be
otherwise circulated in any form of binding or
cover other than that in which it is published and
without a similar condition including this condition
being imposed on the subsequent purchaser.

A CIP catalogue record for this book
is available from the British Library.

ISBN 0 7515 2973 7

Typeset by
Derek Doyle & Associates, Liverpool
Printed and bound in Great Britain by
Clays Ltd, St Ives plc

X Libris
A Division of
Little, Brown and Company (UK)
Brettenham House
Lancaster Place
London WC2E 7EN

# Private Parties

# Chapter One

*SILHOUETTED BY THE* gentle orange light of the fire, the young woman ran a hand slowly down over her waist to her hip. She had a perfect body and she knew as much. Every move she made was calculated to highlight the fact of her perfection and drive all those who saw her wild with lust and desire.

Turning from the fireplace to face the interior of the sumptuous room, she laid a slender arm along the mantelpiece to steady herself as she began the long seductive process of undressing. With her free hand, she began to unfasten the tiny pearlescent buttons of her long white dress, a dress made of a fabric so fine and transparent that it seemed orange where the light of the fire shone through. With each little button that popped easily from its buttonhole, the dress slipped further from the woman's narrow shoulders; smooth brown shoulders that invited caresses or kisses to cover them over again.

'Do you want me to go further?' she asked in a soft, low voice, when the dress was completely open at the front, from delicate neck-line to hem. As if she had to ask ... Taking silence as assent, she rearranged herself at the side of the fireplace, leaning back against the cold wood-panelled wall and putting one foot against it in a casual pose so that her dress fell to either side of her slender body like a carelessly tied dressing gown. Beneath she was wearing a collection of far more exquisite garments than the simple shift that had kept them covered until now. The intricate white lace of a balconette brassière held her perfectly round breasts in gravity-defying beauty. Each time she breathed in, the soft tanned orbs of her bosom seemed to strain against their delicate restraint, silently begging the on-looker to move up behind her and unhook them from their bondage.

'Put some music on,' she commanded. At once the tribal beat of some anonymous band seeped out from the expensive stereo in the corner of the antiques-filled room to fill it like the heady, sexy scent of incense. The woman closed her eyes to fully savour the sensual pleasure of the sound that raised goosebumps on her hot flesh like the breath of a long-desired lover.

'I like this tune,' she purred. 'Make it louder.'

As the sound heightened at her command, the woman casually dipped a long finger into a glass of champagne which stood on the table beside her, and ran a wet line from her cleavage to across the top of her left breast so that the glittering trail emphasised the perfect curve it had followed. Then the woman trailed her finger across her bottom lip, already wet with sticky pink gloss, and winked conspiratorially.

'Tastes delicious,' she murmured, dipping her finger into the glass again. In the flickering firelight the tiny bubbles glittered up to meet her smooth pink fingernail.

This time the woman started a new trail just below the centre of the brassière, where the curved wires that supported her full breasts met, tracing her way down across her ribcage to her flat stomach. Long, narrow and deceptively deep, her tiny navel echoed the promise of another more erotic country still hidden from view. The woman curled her finger around in a tantalising mimicry, before continuing downwards to where the intricate tracery of lace edging her knickers only just covered her pubis. She looked down at herself then with more than a hint of mischief as she edged her fingertip beneath that flimsy boundary of white lace and stroked her silky pubic hair. When she looked up again her eyes were glazed, her pupils dark and fully dilated with a pleasure in her own body that to the onlookers was almost as arousing as her body itself.

'You want to touch me,' she whispered hotly. And she had no reason to doubt that what she said was true.

Throwing back her head so that her long, honey-coloured hair fell tumbling over her shoulders like a silken scarf, she smiled a predatory white-toothed smile as she slid her hand out of her knickers and instead hooked her fingers beneath the taut suspenders which led down across her thighs. She made it seem as though she might at any moment unhook the snowy white stockings that covered her endless legs. Instead she ran her hands all the way up her body again and stretched like a lazy cat, while sliding one narrow foot from the confines of a tottering white shoe that looked as though it had been made to drink champagne from.

Turning her back to the room she stretched languorously and held the folds of her dress out like gossamer butterfly wings so that her body was once more a tantalising shadow of perfection behind a veil of white fabric. The music seemed to grow quieter in anticipation of the moment when she finally slid the dress from her shoulders and let it fall into a shimmering puddle of silk at her spiky heels.

From behind, she was almost more beautiful. As she reached around herself to unhook the gently restraining bra, her fine brown shoulderblades flexed like two tiny angel's wings. The smooth curved line of her spine became a forbidden path that greedy fingers longed to walk and explore. Slowly. Lovingly. The thong back of the white panties she wore separated a pair of soft, pink buttocks that asked to be cheek to cheek with any eager face that wanted to bury itself in her glowing flesh.

Without turning round, the woman took off her bra in one easy move and, twirling it twice around her finger by its strap for effect, tossed the flimsy garment into the room behind her without looking to see where she aimed. It fell like a discarded feather by the ruins of her dress.

Crossing her arms about her chest, she ran her hands along the sides of her body, so that to anyone watching from behind it was as if they were not her own hands but a mystery lover's. The music in the room had slowed again and she began to undulate her hips in time with the lazy beat. She stroked her hands across her peach-skinned buttocks, ran long fingers temptingly over the tops of her stockings and finally, most wonderfully, leaned forward and over to look out from between her perfect legs in a gesture of invitation so explicit that she hardly needed to pull the fabric of her g-string to one side and caress her labia to underline it. But she did.

It might simply have been the champagne still wet upon her finger that glistened in the dying flicker of the firelight, but before anyone could be sure, the woman was gone, disappearing behind the heavy velvet curtain that separated one room from the next before any other hand could touch her; leaving nothing behind but the ghostly fingers of her perfume to caress the empty air.

'Bloody hell,' said Cherry Valentine. 'That was all a bit much, wasn't it?'

'Certainly beats the book launch I went to last week,' agreed her companion, a beer-bellied, middle-aged hack who covered fashion events for the *Chronicle* under the pseudonym 'Melissa Farquharson'.

'What happens next?' Cherry asked him.

'All the guests take their clothes off and start an orgy?' 'Melissa' suggested hopefully.

'What? With the other guests? Not unless there's something much stronger than alcohol in this glass,' said Cherry, recoiling at the thought. 'But the staff? Now that's a different matter altogether. Where do they get them, eh?' she murmured as a black-haired Adonis dressed in nothing but a gold fig-leaf-style thong filled her glass with yet more vintage champagne.

Cherry hadn't expected too much from the launch of Promised Pleasures' new line of lingerie when she pinched the 'exclusive' invitation from the desk of the paper's fashion editor, but as soon as her taxi turned into the gravelled driveway of the venue – a vast but disused country house – and she saw the barely dressed boys and girls at the windows, beckoning the carefully chosen guests inside like a posse of gorgeous young vampires from a Hammer Horror movie, Cherry knew it was going to be fun. She had no idea how much fun, however.

'I think Promised Pleasures can pretty much guarantee a rise in their sales over the next week or so,' Cherry commented. And not a moment too soon. The family-run company had been on the verge of going bust, so to speak, since it had insisted on sticking to its speciality of old-fashioned lace while the rest of the underwear market followed Calvin Klein into the grey jersey formality currently preferred by the British knicker-wearing public.

'Nice to see a return to good old-fashioned values,' nodded 'Melissa', as the model who had just given such good value for money by the fireplace reappeared in a baby-blue ensemble that matched the white one she had pretty much discarded earlier. Hard as Cherry tried, she found it impossible not to stare at the woman's perfect warm curves again as the gorgeous girl positioned herself on the surface of a highly polished dining table with no regard whatsoever for what her spike heels might do to the veneer.

'Here we go again,' said Cherry in mock boredom, as the guests assembled in the dining room suddenly abandoned the nouveau cuisine-style nibbles, which had been placed everywhere but on the dining table, for a far tastier dish.

The honey-blonde lay back on the table, her arms above her head. From somewhere in the dark corners of the room, an unseen *maître d'* with a voice like melting chocolate ran through the elements of 'Caroline's' outfit as she rolled over on to her front and then on to her back again so that everyone could get a proper view of the 'delicate French lace' and 'pure silk gusset'. The onlookers were rapt when she opened her giraffe-long legs to display the 'fine double stitching' between them.

Cherry watched the spectacle for a while, peering from behind a sweaty journalist until she became frustrated by her restricted view. Stepping back from the slightly unpleasant position, she decided that she ought to apply herself to her real job in any case.

Cherry Valentine was a senior reporter for the *Star Times* – a weekly colour supplement, given away free on Saturdays with national tabloid the *Daily Mercury*, that carried a mixture of gossip, reviews and TV listings. Now she cast her jaundiced eye around the Promised Pleasures party to see if she could spot any celebs getting their own share of forbidden fruit. Anyone would do, she told herself. Footballers. Newsreaders. Soap stars behaving badly were best – people loved to read about the incredible contrast between the drab, distressed characters the actors played on TV and the champagne, cocaine and Dolce & Gabbana lifestyles they led when the cameras stopped rolling. But there were no soap stars to be seen that night. At least none in that particular room, which appeared to be full of other members of Cherry's own profession. The ugliest possible members at that, she thought with a sigh.

Taking one last peek at the lovely Caroline over a fellow hack's shoulder, Cherry headed for the door that led from the dining room to the rest of the house. From experience she knew that at this kind of party the celebs were usually protected from the proles in a private VIP room once they had done the obligatory photo-call bit with whatever product was to be pushed. With her sixth sense for such things, Cherry headed up the sweeping staircase in the hallway towards another room from whence more enticing music drifted. As she watched, one of the gorgeous thong-clad waiters from downstairs walked into the room, carrying a bottle of champagne of a much better vintage than the one the hacks had been drinking. Cherry was pretty sure she had struck VIP gold.

She took a deep breath, fluffed up her glossy black bob and prepared to push her way into the private party. When she first started her job at the *Star Times* it had been easy. A pretty girl on her own could wangle her way into just about any event with a wink and a smile, no matter how big and scary the bouncers looked. These days, however, people had started to recognise Cherry from the little picture at the head of her column, and, having put more than a few noses out of joint with some ill-timed or particularly nasty gossip, she had lately found herself on the 'least-wanted' list of many joints. She wasn't going to be put off by the possibility of an unwelcome reception tonight, however. With all these semi-naked models drifting about to encourage bad behaviour in even the saintliest of celebrities, she knew she might be on the verge of a journalist's dream.

But, flinging wide the door to this 'secret room', Cherry found herself not in another party but in a changing room, where the models who prowled the salon downstairs were being dressed and touched up (with concealer, rather than lustful hands). Nevertheless, Cherry snapped a quick photo with her handy compact camera before she backed out again.

Into someone's broad chest.

'Invading people's privacy again?' the man asked archly.

Cherry brushed herself off and straightened up after the shock of the collision. 'Well, what were you intending to do yourself?' she asked. 'Creeping about like some kind of peeping tom.'

'I have an invitation to this private party actually.'

'So do I,' Cherry retorted.

'*Borrowed* no doubt. I could have you thrown out.'

'Then why don't you?' asked Cherry cockily. 'God knows there's no one interesting enough for me to write about in my column here.'

'Why don't you make something up? Isn't that what you usually do?'

Cherry had to smile at that.

The name of the man being so very belligerent was Andreas Eros (not his real name, Cherry suspected) and he was in fact the only celeb she had seen at the party that night. But the popular magician, who modelled himself on the likes of Las Vegas stars David Copperfield and Siegfried and Roy rather than homegrown magic man Paul Daniels, was hardly Cherry's favourite subject. She received a letter from his solicitor every time she so much as breathed his name in the office.

It had started out with a fairly reasonable review of one of his shows. The show had been OK – if you like to see lots of breathing fire and posturing while a couple of miserable-looking Dobermans jump through hoops. Cherry had simply stated that it wasn't her kind of thing, but that throwaway comment was enough to get Mr Eros's ram-rod back up. The only thing was, the angrier Mr Eros got, the more uncharitable Cherry's reviews became. She just couldn't help herself. Of his latest 'erotic magic' show, billed as 'the hottest thing to hit the West End since the Fire of London', Cherry had written that it was as 'sexy as a ham sandwich'. In fact that particular review was due to be published the very next morning. It was a thought which brought a smile to Cherry's lips, even as Eros ranted in front of her now.

'Tell you what,' she said sarcastically. 'Why don't you just wave your big fat wand and make me disappear, eh?' She stood with her hands on her hips as though she was waiting for him to do exactly that.

'If only I could,' Eros snarled back. Then he turned on his Cuban heels and left Cherry alone in the corridor.

She watched him retreat with interest. Much as she had slated his taste in 'slacks' as she disrespectfully referred to them at every opportunity, Eros's dodgy satin trousers really showed off his backside. And it was a pretty impressive backside. She had read in an article written by a rather more respectful journalist that Andreas Eros spent at least two hours a day in a private gym at his country house, keeping his body in peak physical condition for all the prancing about he did in his stage show. After all, no one wants to be upstaged by their dancers or even a couple of well-muscled dogs ... Cherry took a sneaky snap of the perfect posterior with her trusty camera. Might come in handy for a 'rear of the year'-type feature.

'Nice bum, shame about the rest,' she murmured cheekily, just as Eros disappeared into another private room with a defiant toss of his carefully groomed black hair.

'Can I help you, Madam?'

Cherry's daydream about messing up Andreas Eros's slick hairdo was interrupted by the sudden arrival of the black-haired Adonis with the champagne bottle from downstairs. Cherry leaned her head on one side and wondered whether it would be inappropriate to ask him if he could help find her clitoris.

'Could you help me find my clitoris?' she blurted out before she could stop herself. Amazing what a couple of bottles of champagne could do for a girl's self-confidence. (Or for the removal of her inhibitions.) The Adonis smiled slowly and uncertainly and for an awful second Cherry expected him to break into a run.

'I don't think we're supposed to ...' he began.

'I know. But I am the lingerie buyer for every Marks and Spencer store in the land,' Cherry lied quickly. 'I have a seasonal budget that goes into seven figures. I'm sure your bosses would expect you to make an exception for such a valuable potential customer,' she added, though she didn't for one moment expect to get anything more out of him than a smile. A little flirty reciprocation perhaps.

The Adonis bit his lip as he cast a hurried look down the corridor in either direction to see if they were being observed. They weren't; the corridor was completely deserted. The music coming from the main room downstairs suddenly became louder. It was clear that the party was now in full swing and it was unlikely that anyone would come upstairs looking for something better to do just yet.

'We could go up to the attic,' the Adonis said in a whisper.

'Eh?' Cherry's mouth dropped open with surprise.

'None of the guests are supposed to go up there because Promised Pleasures aren't insured for an accident outside the main rooms. I'm not supposed to go up there either in case I fall and hurt my face. I'm a model,' he clarified.

Cherry laughed into her glass. 'Are you serious?'

'What? About being a model? Don't I look like one?' he asked, hurt.

'No. Not about being a model, stupid. About going up into the attic with a total stranger?'

'Yeah. Why not?'

'I was only joking when I suggested it,' she blushed. 'Anything could happen.'

'I hope so,' the Adonis replied, giving her a meaningful stare.

Cherry shuddered delightfully as his gaze seemed to penetrate her clothes. For a moment she wondered what she had started. Perhaps she should be the one to break into a run now.

'I saw you downstairs earlier, watching the show,' he told her as he reached out to caress her face. 'I thought you were really sexy right away, but when I followed you up here to try to get to know you, you were talking to that Andreas Eros bloke. I didn't think I had a chance with you then. Not with his reputation.'

'His reputation?' Cherry sighed as the model ran his hand down the side of her neck.

'Isn't he supposed to be the sexiest man on earth?'

'Purleese,' said Cherry. Her nervousness about trying it on with the model had completely deserted her now. It was as though his smooth hands on her neck had melted it away. 'Andreas Eros is really not my type. Too many . . . clothes,' she said, hooking a finger into the front of the model's gold g-string. 'I think you had better take me to the attic before I change my mind.'

Without hesitation, the model dragged Cherry behind another heavy velvet curtain that hid a narrow, winding staircase leading up into blackness. As soon as they were out of the light of the corridor, he planted his picture-perfect mouth on Cherry's neatly pursed lips and she almost tripped with the shock. By the time they reached the doorway that led to the attic itself, the model, walking behind her, had a hand up her skirt and was already pulling her skimpy panties to one side to get at her most private centre of pleasure.

'Slow down,' she told him, pushing the door open with her shoulder, just as his fingers breached her labia. Once inside the attic she could see him again in the moonlight that crept in through the holes where tiles had once protected the house from the rain. The model-waiter was gorgeous. Like something from a dream. Cherry had never been with a model before and she was thrilled at the thought of adding a new 'first' to her list of experiences. She ran her fingers wonderingly over his beautiful face and felt the thrill of anticipation.

'Better find somewhere safe to stand,' she said, noticing that the floor beneath her feet was almost as full of holes as the roof.

'Over here.' He took Cherry by the hand and led her gingerly through the boxes of junk left behind by the former occupants of the grand house.

A portrait of a stiff-collared man in Victorian dress, probably one of those former occupants, regarded them darkly from a corner of the loft. This wouldn't have happened in his day, Cherry chuckled, as she twanged her new boyfriend's g-string. But then, for one awful moment, she found herself thinking that the stiff old fella in the portrait looked a bit like Andreas Eros, so it was with some relief that she draped her crumpled jacket over the unwanted watcher's frame, while the model, who said between breathless kisses that his name was Aaron, began to struggle with the buttons on her shirt.

As he undressed her, Aaron kissed her hungrily, probing the depths of her mouth with his tongue so erotically that Cherry thought she might come without even getting her knickers off. He tasted of cigarettes and champagne, having doubtless had a glass himself for every one he poured out for the guests. When he took his mouth away from hers to concentrate on her neck, Cherry buried her nose in his thick black hair and breathed in the gorgeous aroma of expensive shampoo and hot male. As he nipped playfully at her neck with his teeth, she dug her neat fingernails into his rock-hard biceps with delight. In the moonlight, the smooth, tanned skin that covered his almost naked body had taken on the appearance of stone and Cherry had a brief, delicious fantasy that she was being seduced by Leonardo Da Vinci's statue of David come to life. With all his working parts hard as marble, she hoped.

Sliding her hands quickly down his back, Cherry sighed with pleasure as she reached the g-string which held Aaron's golden fig-leaf in place. He had unfastened her skirt and pushed it down to her feet so that there were just two g-strings between them where it mattered, his in gold satin, hers in intricate black lace. He had pushed back her black silk shirt so that his bare chest met her breasts in their scanty black covering. The sudden caress of a cool draft of wind through the dilapidated roof was a delicious reminder to Cherry that she was getting naked with a gorgeous man. Just then, she felt the familiar pop of her bra being undone and melted with delight at the feeling of that man's warm hands on her back.

Aaron continued to kiss her frantically as he fondled the twin orbs he had just released. Cherry allowed herself to be taken under his control, her head lolling back in ecstasy as her new lover took each of her nipples between his sharp white teeth and sucked them until they were hard as pebbles. When he moved to kiss her on the lips again, she felt the unmistakable firmness of an eager, raging hard-on beneath the fig-leaf and pressed her pelvis tight against his, pulling him against her by the buttocks, rubbing herself against him until she could no longer resist slipping a hand between their bodies to take hold of his penis.

While she gently pulled Aaron's foreskin back and forth to increase his arousal, he pushed her g-string down over her hips. His girl-soft fingers sought out the musky warmth between her legs, and he slipped one carefully inside. Cherry felt her clitoris swell to attention as Aaron worked at it with the heel of his hand while his long fingers simultaneously stroked the welcoming wetness of her vagina. In her own enthusiastic clutches, Aaron's penis was fast reaching its own peak condition. Breathing hard and in perfect time, the new lovers locked eyes to signal that the moment of ultimate release must surely be about to arrive.

Kicking away her g-string and skirt, Cherry suddenly turned from Aaron and positioned herself with her hands against a low beam. She leaned forward so that her buttocks were tilted invitingly upwards towards him. The intention was unmistakable. Cherry held her breath in anticipation, counting the long hot seconds, until Aaron stepped forward between her parted legs and took her hips firmly and determinedly in his hands.

Cherry gasped as his thick, hard shaft nudged

delicately at the lips of her vagina. Then, unable to wait any longer for her pleasure to begin, she reached back through her legs with her own hand to part her labia and carefully guide him inside.

She drew breath ecstatically as Aaron pushed forward until his pelvis touched her buttocks. He moved slowly at first. Cherry closed her eyes to savour the delicious drag as he pulled his shaft out of her body then pushed in again like a cellist intent on making the strings hum.

But it wasn't long before the power of Aaron's own arousal took control of the rhythm and his tempo increased. Cherry gripped the beam in front of her as she pushed herself back against his urgent movements. Slap. Slap. Slap. The sound of the base of his taut stomach connecting hard with her peachy, curved buttocks seemed loud enough for the whole party to hear.

'Harder,' she shouted joyfully. Aaron's grip tightened around her waist as he hammered his penis home. 'Harder,' she laughed. 'I think I'm going to . . .'

She started to come before she could finish telling him. His gorgeous body; the chilled champagne; the thought of all those glamorous people partying unknowingly beneath their fucking bodies; all collaborated to push Cherry to the edge of pleasure in record time. As her vagina began to pulse and contract with the familiar rhythms of ecstasy, she felt her lover's penis swell to fill her completely, ready to flood her with jets of come that would hit her like exocet missiles.

Cherry's orgasm shot through her body like

electricity, igniting and exciting every nerve it passed until she felt as though she might shake herself apart if she didn't hold on tight. Behind her, Aaron was roaring his approval, pressing his pelvis hard against her round buttocks as his tremendous orgasm jerked out of his body and into hers.

When she looked up through a gap in the roof tiles, Cherry felt sure for one giddy moment that the sky was spinning super-fast above them. Aaron straightened her body up against his and held her close to him, his arms curled around her chest possessively as his penis gave a triumphant dying spurt. His excited panting in Cherry's ear was almost drowned out by the sound of her own blood rushing through her head as her brain put her body on full alert. Aaron continued to hold her against him, wrapping his arms around her aroused swollen breasts, and for just a second it was as though they had known each other for a very long time.

Eventually, however, they had to let go of each other and get back to the party.

'People are getting thirsty down there,' Cherry explained with a slightly regretful smile.

Aaron let his penis slide slowly from her body and gathered her into his arms again for a final kiss. Sweet and delicious. The urgency of their first clash was gone now, but there was still enough warmth between their lips to elicit a tiny eager flicker in the depths of Cherry's stomach.

She retrieved her discarded clothes from the dusty floor of the attic and unveiled the sinister portrait as she put on her jacket. Aaron unhooked his crumpled g-string from the corner of a broken picture frame, where it had ended up in their rush to get naked. As he pulled it back on, Cherry smoothed a hand over his ruffled hair and suggested that they go back downstairs one at a time. 'For decency's sake,' she said.

'One more thing,' Aaron whispered urgently, grabbing her by the wrist as she turned to leave first. She pouted her lips beautifully in anticipation of a request for just one more kiss. But it didn't come.

'You said you were the buyer for Marks and Spencer's lingerie department, right?' Aaron panted. 'Does that mean you can, like, book models for all the fashion shoots too?'

Cherry's smile stiffened as she subtly freed herself from his grasp. 'Sure I can. What's your name again?' she asked.

'Aaron,' he said. 'Aaron Mason.'

'Aiden,' said Cherry distantly. 'I won't forget that.'

Cherry wasn't sure how long she had been upstairs. It hadn't felt like such a long time, but when she got back to the main room where everything had been happening before she left to go celeb-hunting, she found no one but the staff and the models who were variously tidying up and getting dressed again. She didn't bother to hang around and watch. The magic had already started to fade now that the flattering candlelight had been replaced by the buzzing glare of fluorescent strips and the beautiful girls and boys, who had looked so other-worldly in their designer silk underwear, were covered up in the shapeless jeans and jumpers of ordinary life.

Cherry wandered out on to the driveway of the house and lit up a post-coital cigarette. It wasn't until she stood in the cold night air and felt the wind bite through her thin jacket that it struck her that she was now in the middle of nowhere without a lift. She had arrived at the party in a courtesy limousine that had picked her up at the office and dropped her right at the door of the old country house. But there was no courtesy car to be seen now. Cherry wasn't even sure where she was. She hadn't taken much notice of the route her car had taken on the drive out of London, preferring instead to improve her score on the Nintendo Gameboy that she was supposed to have given to her young nephew as a birthday gift.

She fumbled in her bag for her mobile phone, intending to call for a taxi. It was gone. She swore loudly. Come to think of it, she hadn't used it since this morning. It could have been lost or stolen anywhere. Bloody hell. Not that she would have been able to get a signal in this godforsaken place anyway . . .

Cherry turned to go back inside to ask one of the models for the full address of the old house and the number of a cab firm, but the door she had let herself out through only minutes before was now firmly locked against re-entry. As she tried the handle in vain, Cherry heard the sound of a minibus leaving via the back entrance. All the lights in the house had gone out. Cherry realised with annoyance that even the staff had taken their lift and gone.

'Fucking great,' she spat, as she trudged up the driveway towards the road. How long had the trip to the house taken? She tried to remember. It had been at least an hour. Maybe two. She might be as many as a hundred miles from home by now. She wasn't even sure if the journey had taken her north or south.

She had just twisted her ankle in her high-heeled shoes on that stupid gravel path when she found herself caught in the glaring headlights of a passing car. A passing limousine to be precise.

Cherry waved her arms frantically to catch the driver's attention, but he was already drawing up beside her. Perhaps he could radio for one of his mates to come and fetch her, she thought. Even better, perhaps he'd give her a lift back to civilisation himself. She prepared her most seductive grin and leaned in through the passenger window.

'Car from the Promised Pleasures party?' the driver asked. His smart chauffeur's cap completely shaded his eyes, but his full, wide mouth looked friendly enough. He smiled.

'Promised Pleasures?' Cherry echoed dumbly.

The driver nodded.

Thinking quickly, Cherry said, 'Er, yes. That's me. To London, right?'

'I've got the address just here,' said the driver.

'Okay.'

That would do. Cherry got into the car. He didn't have *her* address, of course, but at least he was going back to the city she wanted. She would let him drop her off at the address he had, whoever's address it was, then get the tube back to her own little place in Kilburn. She could only hope that the person who had ordered the car didn't live somewhere ridiculously far south of the Thames.

'Shouldn't take long,' the driver told her. 'Not much traffic at this time of night.'

'Great,' said Cherry flatly. Sinking back into the leather of the back seat, she felt only a momentary pang of guilt for the person who had been left behind without a lift. If there was anybody left behind. The house had looked totally empty to her.

'Mind if I play some music?' the driver asked.

'Go ahead,' Cherry told him. 'As long as it's not Phil Collins.'

'Oh no,' the driver laughed. 'This stuff is magical.'

He pushed a tape into the deck and cranked up the volume. The music that seeped from the speakers wasn't loud though. It was serene, relaxing. A seductive instrumental mix, though Cherry thought that perhaps she could hear a vocal strain buried deep underneath.

'I like that music,' she told the driver.

'So do I,' he answered. 'Puts you in a different frame of mind.'

It had been a long day. Up at six to file the story she should have filed the night before, and then in the office until eight in the evening choosing the best picture of Leonardo DiCaprio in his underwear to illustrate some spurious story she had made up as a feeble excuse to picture him in his pants. Again. Then the party. Those models. All that champagne! Cradled in the caress of the deep leather seat, Cherry soon nodded off and slept soundly all the way back to London. In fact, she only woke up when the car finally stopped outside what she guessed must be the rightful passenger's house.

Jolted awake by the sudden braking of the car,

Cherry looked up in wonder to find herself in Belgravia, outside one of the smartest addresses in town. The buildings were all painted white. Tall and light, they seemed to glow even in the middle of the night, as though the wealthy people who lived within them were just one step down from the angels in heaven. Cherry was hugely relieved that, although she wasn't really that near home, she wasn't south of the river.

'Here you are,' the driver said.

'Yeah, thanks,' said Cherry, struggling to open the door. She wondered whether she should give the driver a tip. She looked in her bag for her purse, but that, like the mobile phone, had gone. Far from giving the driver a tip, she suddenly wondered whether she could ask him for her tube fare home and promise to send him a cheque.

'You'll be needing this,' the driver said, winding down the glass partition between them to give her a single key.

A key? Cherry took it. 'Er, thanks.'

An automatic mechanism somewhere inside the car opened the passenger door and Cherry stepped out on to the pavement. The limousine sped away instantly, and almost silently. The driver hadn't even wished her goodnight, which made Cherry feel slightly embarrassed. She wondered if she had offended him. Had she snored? Or even talked in her sleep as he drove? Cherry's last lover had warned her that she talked as she dreamt, and right then she had the awful feeling that she'd been dreaming pretty vividly about having sex and might have been acting out her part in the dream. The music he had been playing in the car had been the perfect erotic soundtrack.

Whatever, Cherry thought. No point being embarrassed now. She wouldn't have to see the driver again.

She rubbed her tired eyes and looked at the key in her hand. If only it had been a two pound coin, she mused. Then she might have been able to get on the tube and hurry home to her own bed.

Cherry walked as far as the end of the block before looking back at the house the driver had brought her to. Unlike most of the other houses in the street, it was completely dark; not even a light in the porch to suggest someone's imminent return. Cherry thoughtfully turned the key over in her chilly hand. She ought at least to push it through the letterbox, she mused. It wouldn't be right to just walk off with the key to someone else's home. She couldn't steal someone's lift *and* their key.

But just as she opened the letterbox to put the key through, Cherry decided that she really ought to see whether it actually fitted the lock – to make sure that she had the right house, of course. And perhaps it wouldn't be so awful if she went so far as to see whether the lucky person who owned this gorgeous house was the kind of person who also kept change in a bowl by the door for the milkman, or the odd passing society columnist who didn't have her tube fare home.

A jet black cat sitting on the doorstep of the house seemed almost to nod in agreement.

## Chapter Two

*THE FRONT DOOR* creaked open slowly, as though it hadn't been used in a while. The entrance lobby of the grand house smelled musty too, confirming Cherry's first impression. When she flicked the nearest light switch, the bulb flared only briefly before popping and plunging her back into darkness. There was just enough light from the street outside to show that unopened letters littered the tiled floor, most of it junk mail – menus from pizza delivery firms and mini-cab cards. Cherry called out a nervous 'hello' but was answered only by the slightly mournful echo of her own voice. And there was no sign of the pot full of loose change she had hoped for either.

She was about to turn and leave when she felt something slink past her leg. She shrieked before she looked down and saw the tail of a cat flick around the edge of the interior door. Realising that it must have been the cat that had been waiting outside on the pavement, Cherry felt her body slacken in relief. No ghosts here. She let herself back out on to the street, locked the door, and was again about to post the key through the letterbox when she realised that there was every possibility that the cat was just as much a trespasser as she had been.

Cherry bit her lip. Chances were that the cat did actually belong to the owner of the house. But if it didn't, by locking the door behind her, she could be condemning the cat to starvation and perhaps even death. Judging by the pile of mail in the hallway, the house hadn't been opened for weeks. What if no one came by for another few weeks? By that time the cat would certainly have died. And much as she hated the flea-ridden things, Cherry couldn't bring herself to walk away and leave it to its fate.

Groaning at the sudden complication, Cherry unlocked the door again and called to the cat. Predictably, it didn't reappear like the well-trained moggy she had hoped for.

Growing bolder, she kicked a pile of takeaway leaflets aside and picked her way forward carefully. She would have to go further inside. In any case, she convinced herself, now that she had technically broken into the house, she might as well see what lay beyond the dark hallway. Ever the sleuth, she told herself. Nosy, was what her mother called it.

She found the kitchen first. In a pool of orange light from the street outside, a basket of what must once have been fruit sent a hideous bouquet of decay spiralling up from the table; further confirmation that the house had been abandoned for quite some time. There was a card with the basket, but it bore only the name of the delivery service, no clue as to who might have sent or received it. Cherry shuddered at the sight of the furry mould that had gathered on an ancient orange. An open box of chocolates next to the basket looked almost perfect however. Cherry plucked a foil-wrapped truffle and felt like Goldilocks in the house of the Three Bears, stealing a bite of the metaphorical porridge. Might as well go and try the beds out, she told herself.

She climbed the grand, if slightly shabby, staircase to the first floor. Moonlight flooded in through a dirty skylight to illuminate a white-painted landing that led to three further rooms behind huge white-painted doors. The first was a sitting room where an antique grand piano stood covered by a sheet, unplayed for years judging by the dust. Cherry lifted the sheet and sounded a single mournful note, before she remembered that she was in fact trespassing in a stranger's house and thought better of playing a quick tune.

'Puss,' she called instead. 'Come here, pussykins.' If she was going to get caught traipsing through someone's home uninvited, she needed to make sure her excuse was realistic. But the cat wasn't hiding beneath the piano.

From the wall of the next room, where there was no furniture at all beneath which a cat could hide, a series of grim portraits glared down at the intruder. Cherry stood in front of a painting of a woman who had more chins than the fat chow dog pictured sitting on her lap and tried to find a family resemblance with any of the rich Belgravians she knew. Could even be royalty with chins like that, she thought. The portrait of a man, hanging on the opposite wall, was more familiar however. It reminded Cherry of the portrait in the attic at the Promised

Pleasures party. And thinking of the attic reminded her of Aaron.

Remembering his muscular chest against her own and his tight brown buttocks beneath her palms, Cherry closed her eyes and slid her hand slowly between her legs. She could still feel the burn left by that short but sweet encounter. One of her all time top ten shags perhaps, she thought to herself wickedly. Cherry winked at the disapproving portrait as she slotted the lovely Aaron in at a mental number eleven, behind the man who had come to fix a leak in her bathroom and stayed to test out the power shower *à deux*.

Leaving the portraits with that lascivious thought, Cherry continued her explorations. The third room on that landing contained a bed. Cherry almost gasped with awe when she saw the four poster in the middle of the floor. It was huge. Heavy, red silk curtains embroidered with flowers and exotic birds hung from the dark oak canopy that concealed a den of mismatched silken pillows. She pressed down on the mattress with both hands to see how firm it was before she kicked off her shoes, climbed on to the bed and lay down. She surprised herself. It was as though she felt suddenly compelled to do it. Absolutely compelled. Just for a moment, she told herself, as she spread out her limbs luxuriously. Just a little dream. Then she'd continue her search for that cat.

Cherry had always wanted a four poster bed. Hasn't every girl? Relaxing back on to the jumble of pillows she recalled a thousand fairy stories. Sleeping Beauty. The Princess and the Pea. Hasn't every girl at some point or another wanted to be the princess; rescued from a life of poverty or a wicked witch's spell by a handsome prince who would shower her with gifts and attention? Cherry Valentine didn't need rescuing from anything, of course, but that wasn't to say that she would have minded having someone try.

As she gazed up into the almost organic swags and folds of the bed's tented canopy, Cherry recalled hearing that in the original story of Sleeping Beauty, the heroine is awoken not with a kiss, but with the act of penetration. Must have been a bit of a shock for the virgin princess, Cherry thought, but it was something she had often thought about since first hearing what really happened in the Grimm fairytale. These days, a great deal older and more experienced than the young girl who had listened open-mouthed to fairytales, Cherry was quite enamoured of the idea of waking to find a handsome lover already on top of her. Waking with an orgasm perhaps. Now that had to be infinitely preferable to waking to the sound of a Wallace and Gromit alarm clock.

This fantasy awakening would have to take place in a four poster bed, of course. Cherry looked up at the exquisitely embroidered canopy overhead, slipped her hand beneath the narrow waistband of her skirt and beneath the black lace of her g-string. She sought out her clitoris, still slightly swollen from Aaron's enthusiastic attentions, and began to stroke it gently. It wasn't long before her body was stirring once more with the arousal emanating from that centre. Each long stroke of Cherry's own fingers seemed to send another wave of heat flooding through her lower body, pushing the warmth she was generating a little further along her limbs so that soon she no longer felt the chill in that drafty room.

With her free hand, she gently caressed her round breasts through her crumpled black silk blouse. She tried to imagine that her soft warm hands were not part of her own body but the hands of a mysterious lover. Over the years she had built up a picture of this strange prince of dreams that she stored at the back of her mind. She thought about him less and less as she grew older and met more frogs than princes in London's clubs and pubs, but when she wanted to, Cherry could conjure up her dream lover in perfect detail.

He would be tall, of course. At least as tall as she was. He would have shoulders so wide that he blocked out the light when he stood in the doorway. He would have big muscular arms with sinews like knotted ropes and strong hands roughened by hard work. He would be able to lift her from the bed as though she weighed no more than a feather, and yet at the same time he would be able to administer pleasure to her longing body with the delicacy of a virtuoso pianist.

Cherry imagined her dream lover kneeling on the bed between her legs now. Imagined him dipping his beloved head so that his thick black curls (he always had black hair) obscured his noble face from view. His face had changed over the years as she met different men who intrigued and inspired her, but right then it wasn't important. Cherry didn't need to see his wolf-like grey eyes or run her finger down his sculpted cheek. For now her pleasures were more tactile. She imagined the delicious feel of his hot tongue as he touched it gently against her clitoris; his big hands grasping her shaking thighs to keep them still as he licked the shell-pink inner surface of her labia until she felt sure that she would pass out from joy.

And then, when she thought that she could take no more, her prince would climb on top of her and take her absolutely. She would put up no resistance as his penis slid slowly inside her vagina. She would close her eyes and offer herself up to pleasure totally as he rocked his body against hers. She felt as though she had been waiting for a hundred years for just that ultimate moment.

Cherry's dream lover would know exactly how to bring her to the most fantastic orgasm of her life. He would know exactly when to speed up his rocking, when to slow down and take things more gently. Faster then more slowly, fast then slow. He would know exactly how to move so that her pleasure built gradually in intensity like ocean waves heading for the shore. Until the seventh wave came and she would be able to hold back no longer . . .

She shuddered as her orgasm sent her body into an involuntary dance of joy. When the seventh wave had retreated again, she felt perfectly at peace with herself. Calm. She felt as though every cell in her being had been caressed, stroked, becalmed. All the anxiety of her day-to-day existence had been washed away in that moment and for a short while Cherry felt as though she was floating above the sumptuous bed on a cloud of happiness. She may have brought herself to orgasm on a fantasy but the orgasm itself had been real enough. Lying on a stranger's bed, Cherry rolled over on to her side and hugged her knees against her body as though she were hugging her dream lover to sleep.

She was almost nodding off when a soft, almost feather-like caress on her cheek brought her back to wakefulness again.

She sat up suddenly, and in fright, as it came to her in a second that she was lying in a strange house on a stranger's bed. She threw herself on to the floor to escape her discoverer, but it wasn't any human being who had touched her cheek. Cherry felt her body crumple in relief when she realised that the cat she had seen sitting outside the house had been making itself at home on the pillow beside her.

'You frightened me,' she admonished the sleek black creature. 'I thought you were the lady of the house.'

But despite her relief, once the thought that she was trespassing had crossed Cherry's mind again, it didn't seem like such a good idea to hang around any longer. What had she been doing? Bringing herself off like that when she could have been walked in on at any moment? Cherry searched beneath the bed for her discarded shoes and slipped them on hurriedly. Whether or not anyone was going to come home to the house that night, it was time for Cherry to go.

'Come on, mog,' she whispered to the cat. 'Time for you to go too.'

She reached out and picked up the cat from its comfy place on the pillow. 'You don't want to be locked in an empty house.'

The cat seemed to purr in agreement, but before

Cherry could reach the bottom of the stairs with the furry bundle of trouble in her arms, the cat wriggled free again and made a run for it. Unfortunately, it didn't make a run in the direction of the front door.

Cherry's own breathing was loud in her ears as she stared at another half-open door leading from the echoing stairwell. She didn't remember the door to the cellar being open when she had walked through the hallway before, but she had to convince herself that it must have been open, just to be able to keep breathing and not keel over in fright.

'Puss,' she called weakly.

The stupid cat had run down into the cellar. Should she leave the pesky animal and go? That certainly seemed the sensible option when faced with the prospect of going down into the dark to fetch it. Cherry had a natural horror of cellars. But she also knew that she would only spend the rest of the night worrying that she had left the poor cat to starve to death trapped in a deserted house if she didn't see it safely back on to the street.

Breathing heavily, Cherry pushed the door gingerly. Like the front door, it creaked in protest after many months of disuse. She felt along the dark wall just inside the door for a light switch. Thank goodness the bulb stayed lit this time – not that the yellowing orb did a particularly good job of illuminating the narrow dusty staircase which led down to yet more darkness.

'Come on, cat,' Cherry called from the top of the stairs, trying to sound more confident than she felt right then. 'Don't do this to me. I want to be getting home.'

Cherry was about to give up when a faint mew called back. She bit her lip. 'Oh, God. I bet you've gone and got yourself stuck in something, haven't you? I suppose I'd better come down.' She tried to say it lightly, needing to break the silence to give herself courage, but her voice wavered with nerves.

'I hate small, dark places,' she confided to the silence of the house.

She took off her high-heeled shoes to negotiate the stairs – and to jam the cellar door open so that it didn't slam behind her – cursing with frustration as she snagged the fragile soles of her stockings on splinters with every step. When she reached the bottom of the short flight she peered out into the darkness. The echo of her own nervous cough told her that she was standing in quite a large room, but only a small circle of the dusty floor was lit by the light from the stairs. Cherry called to the cat again and was answered with another feeble mew.

'For God's sake,' she grumbled as she waited for her eyes to become accustomed to the light, or rather the lack of it. 'Where are you?'

After a few minutes or so of frustrated straining to make out the shape of a cat in the gloom, Cherry remembered that she had a lighter in her bag. She took it out and, moments later, its weedy flame cast long wavering shadows on to the walls of the cellar.

And what walls they were. Cherry blinked to make sure that she wasn't seeing things. The pathetic glow cast by the lighter had illuminated a room far more sumptuous than the rooms above the stairs. A room more beautiful in fact than any Cherry had seen in her years traipsing through the fantastic homes of the rich and famous to get a decent photo story for her magazine. It was as though the tall white house, that had seemed so neglected, hid the remains of an ancient temple, for the terracotta-coloured walls of the cellar were covered in scenes from ancient mythology that looked as though they had been in place for thousands of years.

This bizarre discovery momentarily overcame Cherry's fear of cellars – she had expected spiders and cobwebs, dirt and dangerously connected wiring, but instead found herself in a room that looked as though it had been transported wholesale from a palace. Holding her lighter aloft, Cherry drifted around the room from painting to painting. As she looked more closely, she realised that the scenes represented in this room were not taken from mythology at all. At least, not mythology as she had come to know it from history lessons at her all-girls' secondary school. Rather, they were scenes from some kind of Romanesque Kama Sutra.

Cherry cocked her head on one side to examine a pastoral scene in which a beautiful woman dressed in nothing but gold chains and a serene smile was being attended by three men. Her legs were raised so that you could see where one of the men was impaling her with a long thin cock. In the next scene, another smooth-faced man thrust an only slightly shorter, thicker cock into the same woman's luscious open mouth. She was pleasuring the third man with her narrow, bejewelled hands.

'Exhausting,' Cherry murmured.

Another picture showed a young black guy, with a chest as wide as a door, chained to some kind of stake, while young men and girls armed only with long peacock feathers stroked him into ecstatic submission. The muscles on his chest were well defined as he strained backwards to avoid their tickling. His penis, Cherry noted with a mixture of shock and amusement, was as long and thick as a horse's.

Another painting portrayed the same man, this time tugging fiercely at his own penis as one of the girls who had been teasing him so cruelly with a feather lay back across a stool decorated with carved tigers' feet as she allowed herself to be taken by a man with what appeared to be a goat's hindquarters instead of human legs. Not that that seemed to be adversely affecting the young girl's enjoyment. Her face was a picture of pleasure. Though her eyes were screwed tightly shut, they were tipped up at the corners, echoing the beneficent curve of her mouth, as if she might be laughing as she came.

The next frieze was even more intriguing. Cherry peered closely at the portrayal of a beautiful woman allowing a noble-faced man to fondle her perfect little breasts. And yet another man to suck on her penis simultaneously . . . Cherry did a double-take. The beautiful woman was in fact a hermaphrodite.

Cherry felt a peculiar frisson at this discovery. She had often wondered whether such a creature had ever existed. A penis and a vagina. A woman's breasts rising above a young man's rippled abdomen. The hermaphrodite's delicate genitals looked like the bud of some rare exotic flower.

'Best of both worlds,' Cherry murmured as she studied the hermaphrodite's ecstatic face and subconsciously let her own hand drift towards her pubis.

Looking up from the walls, she was greeted by a star-scape. The black-painted ceiling of the basement room was studded with tiny pieces of mirrored glass that glittered back the light of her cheap cigarette lighter and turned it into something magical. The shards of glass were laid out in a pattern that reflected the constellations. Cherry recognised the Plough, of course. She was trying to find Venus when behind her, a sudden noise demanded her attention.

Cherry whirled around to face the black cat, which was making itself at home on another bed and had knocked over a candlestick in the process. Cherry clutched at her throat until her nerves subsided again. She picked up the candle and lit it from her lighter. It didn't make much difference, just cast even longer shadows that seemed to reach out to touch her when she wasn't looking. Cherry scooped the cat up once more.

'We've got to go,' she told him firmly. 'I can't take any more scares tonight.'

But with the cat now in her arms, she noticed that where he had been sitting, a tiny box lay on the mattress. It was a wooden box, not much bigger than a matchbox, and inlaid with highly-polished pieces of shell that gave it the air of being something more precious than it probably was. Nothing special, but it drew Cherry back to the bed.

Sitting down in the warm dip left by the cat, Cherry picked the box up and looked at it carefully. It was familiar somehow, and almost without thinking, she flicked the little hidden catch that opened a secret compartment. At the same time she remembered exactly where she had seen a box like that before.

It had been a long time ago. A hot summer holiday. Cherry was taking a break between finishing school and starting university and, desperately trying to scrape together the cash to go on a wild weekend in France before she left to start her degree, she had taken a job as a magician's assistant. The magician, who called himself the Great Lorenzo, wasn't Cherry's ideal choice of boss – he was a fiftysomething perv with a wall-eye and wandering hands – but in Cherry's little seaside town, it was a toss up between wearing a bright pink leotard and laughing at an old man's jokes or cleaning the loos in a chintzy b.&b. Besides, magicians' assistants weren't expected to be up before noon.

Cherry would roll into work at the end of pier theatre, just as everyone else was on their way home from their boring offices, and begin her duties by checking the magician's equipment for that evening. There wasn't much to check. The Great Lorenzo's stock-in-trade was more sleight of hand and card tricks than sawing girls in half. Before each show in the tiny theatre, Cherry spent an hour or so stuffing diaphanous scarves back into secret compartments, from whence they would be miraculously magicked later on, and cleaning out the cage belonging to Lorenzo's one live prop – a rabbit called Hector. Hector had a perpetually harrassed expression which wasn't surprising considering that he was pulled from a hat by his ears once a night.

The Great Lorenzo had also had a little box like the one Cherry now held in her hand. For the purposes of the show, he would invite members of the audience to donate rings and bracelets that would be placed in the box to be mysteriously magicked away, then magicked back again just as sighs of surprise were replaced by worried frowns. Off-stage, Lorenzo would ask Cherry to lend him a pound coin, put it in the box, then, when she went to look in the box, he would flick open the secret compartment to show that it held, not her coin, but a Durex. He did it at least once a week. 'I'll double your wages,' he'd mutter with a wink. And Cherry always slapped him for his trouble. When she left to start her university course, the Great Lorenzo gave her the magic box as a parting gift. 'To give you dreams of me,' he'd said with a weird smile as he pressed the little present into her hands. She had quickly passed it on to someone she didn't even remember now, though as she held this new box in her hand the faintest recollection of a stranger's face entered her mind; soft lips kissing hers in thanks. Cherry tried to catch the fleeting memory but couldn't.

Strange to see a cheap box of tricks like that in a place like this; a room where someone had obviously gone to a lot of trouble or expense to recreate a little piece of a palace. In fact, the box's incongruous presence had been almost comforting in the unfamiliar room, and when Cherry replaced it exactly as she had found it, a sense of unease came over her again.

She had a feeling that in coming into this painted cellar she had stumbled upon the centre of someone's most secret life. And while, as a journalist, her *raison d'être* was to uncover secrets (and the darker the better, of course), Cherry suddenly felt as though this was something that she couldn't use to her advantage.

With the cat in her arms and the candle held out precariously to light her way, she felt compelled to whirl around and look at the painted walls. As she moved, the pictures seemed to move as well. The randy goat-boy fucked the sweet-faced girl. The young black guy writhed against his restraining post. The beautiful hermaphrodite seemed to let her head roll back in ecstasy as eager tongues touched her lotus-like genitalia again and again.

But whenever Cherry tried to focus; to catch the girl with the peacock feather drawing it tantalisingly down the captive guy's sweating body, or the goat-boy withdrawing his penis so far that you could see the light glance off the sweet stickiness on its shaft, the pictures froze again and became what they were. Just pictures. Only the flickering of the candlelight and the glittering of the mirrors embedded above her in the ceiling had brought the scenes to life. There was nothing truly animate in that room but Cherry and the cat she cradled in her arms.

At that moment, the cat stiffened as if it had heard something that was beyond Cherry's senses. Its yellow eyes widened and it flattened its velvet pointed ears back against its skull. Cherry didn't wait to find out what had made the cat take fright.

Slamming the front door of the house shut behind her, she set the cat down on the pavement and, without putting her shoes back on in case her high heels slowed her down, hurried off into the night. At the end of the street, she paused to look both ways for traffic. It was then, inexplicably, that she felt herself drawn to look back in the direction she had come. When her eyes fell upon the lonely white house, Cherry thought she saw a light at one of the upstairs windows. She took two more steps before she looked back again. This time the light was gone. Cherry wrapped her jacket tightly around her and tried to convince herself that in looking back she had focused on the wrong house. It was the only explanation.

# Chapter Three

*FINALLY, COCOONED IN* her own bed later that night, Cherry closed her eyes but couldn't sleep. Every creak, every whispered sigh of the winter wind outside her rattling sash window had her flicking her eyes wide open again like an up-ended china doll. She couldn't shake off a feeling of intense unease. It was as if something had followed her from that house and was waiting for her to fall asleep before it pounced.

She knew it wasn't possible. She had seen no one at all between the white house and her own. It had been such a ridiculously long walk as well. Anyone intent on harming her would surely have given up following after the first half hour. Cherry put her uneasy feelings down to guilt. She had been raking through someone's most private possessions uninvited.

Giving up on dropping off, Cherry climbed out of bed again and walked around her little flat. She made herself a drink, and tried to watch some TV on the ancient portable set that graced her bedside table. In fact, it was while she was watching coverage of some boring golf tournament on the other side of the world, that sleep finally enfolded her in its arms.

Since she had closed the door on that creepy house, disturbing images had been scraping on the hatch of Cherry's unconscious mind with their chilly hands. When she finally relaxed into sleep they crept out almost immediately. A swirling mist of colour gave birth to shapes that formed into vaguely remembered silhouettes.

First came the girl with the peacock feather, dressed in a soft white scarf so incredibly fine that it served only to emphasise rather than conceal her voluptuous curves. As she stepped out of the mist, her dark eyes twinkled as she stroked her plump top lip with the tip of the shimmering feather and smiled. Her smile was an invitation to join her; the downward cast of her eyes hinted at sexual undertones.

Gradually, the paintings from the hidden room became a real, three-dimensional world inside Cherry Valentine's sleeping mind. Suddenly, she could feel the soft caress of the warm wind floating in from the sea across the Italian countryside, bringing with it the delicate scent of flowers and olive trees. Grapes ripening on their vines. The hot scent of her own sun-kissed skin.

Birds with unfamiliar voices called to each other from hidden vantage points in the lush green foliage of the tall cypress trees that lined the path Cherry found herself upon. A spotted deer, its silky ears twitching to catch any hint of danger on the breeze, stepped slowly across the scene on slender legs that seemed too delicate to carry even its negligible weight.

Looking down, Cherry was surprised to see that her own feet were strapped into a pair of gilded leather sandals. The thongs wound up across her ankles on to taught calves brown from the sun. As she watched, her arms were suddenly encircled by delicate golden bangles that wrapped her from wrist to elbow like a metallic vine around a tree. When she put her hand up to her soft black hair, she discovered that tiny flowers were woven into the intricate design of her new style. Around her voluptuous body, she was wearing a fine white scarf identical to that worn by the girl with the peacock feather who beckoned her now from behind a tree. Without hesitating, Cherry followed the girl to a walled garden, knowing what she would find behind the wall as cries of joy and ecstatic pain drifted towards them.

She was right. Just as in the paintings in the hidden room, a young black man stood against a slender tree trunk that had been stripped of its branches, while three girls danced around him laughing, binding him tightly to the trunk with thin ropes and strips of leather. The man was completely naked but for a bangle around one wrist. His wide chest glistened with sweat and his thighs were tensed hard against his bondage. Yet although he was very much a prisoner of the girls who danced around him, he couldn't stop himself from breaking into a smile brighter than the hot sun that beat down on his head whenever one of them touched him.

'Melissa,' cried the man when he saw Cherry's beautiful companion appear in the courtyard.

Gesturing that Cherry should follow, Melissa ran to join her friends. When they had finished smothering her with kisses of greeting, Melissa suddenly dropped to her knees in front of their prisoner and took his penis into her mouth as naturally as if she was about to take a drink from a fountain. The other girls giggled and cheered their encouragement. Cherry stepped forward nervously.

Melissa pursed her lips into a loose oval shape and allowed the prisoner's penis to drag out slowly across them, then she sucked the shaft back in again. She took the penis in so far it seemed that it must have been going down the back of her long, fine throat. At the same time, she gently cupped the man's soft testicles in her delicate hands. She repeated this sequence of movements more and more quickly until, above her bobbing head, the man's face contorted with joy. But just as he was getting really excited, Melissa let his penis drag slowly out across her lips one more time before she straightened up and left the shaft pointing unsatisfied and aimless into the warm summer air.

She stood up and beckoned to Cherry once more. The other girls grinned at Cherry and she smiled back in confusion. What did they want her to do? With a gesture of slight impatience, Melissa took Cherry by the arm and led her forward until she was standing with her pubic bone almost touching the chained man's penis.

The flimsy scarf Cherry had been wearing until now was held across her pelvis by a golden chain of a belt. Melissa pulled the section of scarf that dangled between Cherry's legs to one side and invited her to climb on to the chained man's erect penis.

Dumbstruck, Cherry hesitated, but Melissa wrapped an arm around her shoulders and subtly urged her forwards again.

'He's yours now,' Melissa whispered. 'Your turn.'

Not knowing quite what she was doing, Cherry raised herself shakily on to her tip-toes and, placing her hands on the man's shoulders, moved forwards so that his shaft was between her shaking legs. But she wasn't to let him penetrate her, the other girls made that much clear. Melissa motioned to Cherry that she should just slide backwards and forwards along the shaft's shimmering length, allowing herself to be stimulated by the friction against her labia, but not allowing the prisoner any chance of full release.

At first, Cherry felt slightly nervous of performing such a task in front of these strangers, but the other girls gathered behind her and laughed their encouragement as she moved. Between her legs, Cherry felt the captive man's shaft twitch and harden further. His kind brown eyes were fixed on hers, begging her to allow him to reach his climax, but Melissa and her friends forebade that. In any case, Cherry was surprised to find that she didn't need him to be inside her. Not yet.

Hidden beneath the glossy triangle of her pubis, Cherry's clitoris began to hum and throb with the exquisite arousal produced by the friction of her body against the man's shaft. The soft skin on the inside of her slim thighs began to tingle as rays of pleasure spread throughout her body again. She gripped the chained man's shoulders tightly and moved faster. Cherry could tell from his laboured breathing that he was ready to come when two of the other women hurriedly pulled her away.

Almost panting herself, Cherry held the man's dark brown eyes with her own as yet another woman took over the task of continuing this grand tease. With professional skill, the new woman tugged the man's balls downwards gently before she mounted him. A short tug, but it was enough to stop him from letting go. With proper control, Melissa explained, these girls could keep their prisoner hard enough for their purposes for hours. There were six girls around the post where he was tethered now, and they each wanted to have their turn before the man was finished.

'Follow me,' Melissa whispered.

Cherry reluctantly followed her guide, in her chinking bangles and tinkling ankle chains, away from the captive man. Cherry's appetite had been aroused now. As she ran to keep up with Melissa, who was now leading her through the endless rooms of a cool marble palace, her every step transferred delightful pressure to her engorged labia.

As they moved through the dream palace, the walls of the corridors shimmered as though seen through a heat haze. Cherry felt the wind flutter like warm fingers across her body. Distant laughter seemed to mock her when she turned right in Melissa's footsteps only to find that the girl was suddenly beckoning from a doorway to the left. It was as though they were racing through a hall of mirrors that made it impossible to know whether they were heading east, west, north, south or just round and round in circles.

It seemed as though they had been through a hundred rooms before Melissa came to a halt by a heavy, carved door. She ran her hands lustfully over the relief figures of a man and woman twining around each other like the grape vines in the steep fields outside the palace. Then Melissa took Cherry's own hand and placed it on that part of the carving where the man's long penis, gleaming from the polish of a thousand hands over the years, entered the woman's flower-like vagina. Cherry's guide smiled broadly as their eyes met.

'For love,' Melissa murmured. Then she pushed open the door and pulled Cherry into the room after her.

It was almost pitch black. Melissa grabbed a torch from a holder beside the door and held it up towards the ceiling as they entered. As in the secret room below the stairs of the white house, the ceiling in this room was studded with mirrors that mimicked the stars in the heavens. Melissa moved her torch about above her head, mesmerising Cherry with the glittering patterns she created. Tiny shards of light fell everywhere: on the deep red-painted walls; on Cherry's upturned face; on the bodies of the oblivious lovers entwined on a bed piled high with silk-covered pillows where moments earlier there had been no one.

'Sssh,' Cherry's companion put her finger to Cherry's surprised lips and pulled her towards the camouflage of a dark corner.

The couple on the bed didn't seem to have noticed that they were not alone. They continued to slide over and under each other, kissing, stroking, licking. Cherry held herself as still as the carving on the ancient door, acutely aware of every move or sound her sweltering body made. Suddenly even her breathing seemed inordinately loud. It didn't seem possible that the lovers hadn't noticed their presence. She wanted the walls to swallow her up, and when she leaned back against them, she almost felt as though they would oblige.

Cherry's companion was less shy. In the feeble light of the torch, Cherry could see that Melissa was watching the couple intently, her big eyes darting quickly across the writhing bodies, sucking every detail in greedily. When she pushed her thick dark hair back from her eyes to see even more, Melissa's bangles seemed to crash together like cymbals. But the lovers didn't let that interrupt their congress.

Noticing Cherry's hesitancy, Melissa nodded her head vigorously in the direction of the bed. This time her long, intricate earrings jangled like church bells and the lovers did look over to see who had joined them. When she locked eyes with Cherry, however, the woman on the bed merely smiled and nodded.

The woman was sitting astride the prone body of the naked man, and she laughed softly as she inched her way backwards along the length of his firm thighs so that his penis stood proudly in front of her like the tethering pole in the courtyard. As Cherry watched with widening eyes, the woman took her lover's engorged penis in her hand and stroked the foreskin back and forth almost casually while the man fondled her full round breasts in return.

'Would you like me to suck you now?' the woman asked in a whisper.

The man nodded eagerly, and the woman quickly shuffled backwards along his legs to find a position which would make it easier for her to reach his penis with her mouth. Now the woman's perfect bottom was raised in the air and Cherry was glad of the darkness of the room as she stared at the tight bare buttocks.

Between those peachy orbs, a darkly inviting slit already glistened with the juices of arousal. As the woman sucked enthusiastically at the growing shaft she held tightly in one hand, she pushed her other hand between her own legs to stroke her clit simultaneously. Cherry was frozen with amazement as she watched the woman pleasure both herself and her partner with her long-nailed fingers and plump red lips.

Cherry was so absorbed in the spectacle that it was a while before she noticed that her guide had been drawing closer to her all the while. Insinuating herself into Cherry's space little by little, Melissa eventually stretched out an elegant arm and laid it gently around Cherry's smooth shoulders. Cherry opened her mouth to say something, but again Melissa put a finger to her lips in case she broke the spell of silence that had enabled the couple on the bed to be so uninhibited in their presence.

Back on the bed, the woman dragged the tip of her long middle finger lazily down the length of her glistening vagina. Cherry felt her own, still tingling, vagina contract sympathetically at the sight, and when Melissa wrapped her arm around Cherry's waist and turned Cherry's face towards her own for a kiss, Cherry was surprised to discover that she felt more than ready to join the erotic dance.

It started so very gently. Melissa pressed her full red lips against Cherry's pinker ones with a touch as light and gentle as a butterfly landing on a rose. Then she placed a row of smaller, more tender kisses along Cherry's top lip first, and then the bottom one, before following these teasing kisses with a languorous lick that took in the whole of Cherry's mouth. Next, Melissa took Cherry's upper lip between her warm lips and sucked at it, hard. Cherry felt a tugging sensation deep inside her stomach which she recognised instantly as the signal her body gave her when something or someone was turning her on.

'The Kama Sutra teaches us that the channel in a woman's upper lip sends signals directly to the clitoris,' Melissa murmured. And as if by magic, Cherry was sure she felt a pathway of energy open up within her at the very thought.

Melissa took Cherry's upper lip in her mouth again, but this time she completed the circuit of sexual energy by placing her hand directly over Cherry's vagina as she sucked. As her clitoris swelled to attention beneath Melissa's warm and expert fingers, Cherry thought she could feel the channel from lip to clitoris open up again. Certainly, all through the centre of her body, she suddenly felt as if there ran a pathway of heat, like molten lava escaping from a long dormant volcano. The lava was spreading insistently to every part of her body. The tips of Cherry's fingers tingled as she placed her own hands gingerly on Melissa's smooth brown shoulders and gripped the soft flesh there to steady herself.

With her free hand, Melissa began to massage one of Cherry's breasts with the same mesmerising rhythm she was using on her vagina. The deep red walls of the room around them softened and even seemed to pulsate as Cherry allowed herself to give in to the extraordinary and novel sensations her new lover was arousing all the time.

She opened her mouth to allow Melissa's tongue inside again. Melissa ran it first over Cherry's teeth before thrusting it up against the roof of Cherry's mouth. As she did so, Melissa echoed the action by thrusting a single finger deep inside Cherry's vagina. Cherry stiffened momentarily at the invasion, but Melissa quickly relaxed her with murmured words.

'I'll be gentle with you,' she promised.

Cherry registered the calming voice through a rush of blood to her ears. Blood was rushing everywhere. The extremities of her awakening body tingled with its welcome heat, and her skin radiated yet more into the heavy atmosphere of the room as a blush of arousal spread across her breasts and up her neck to her cheeks. Eventually, Cherry was sure she could feel each individual root as her hair stood to attention.

Laughing softly at Cherry's half-hearted sighs of discomfort, Melissa increased the frequency of her frigging at Cherry's clit. Cherry almost forgot to breathe as the sensations intensified. She felt as though her body was being immersed in a ball of fire. This must be what it feels like to burn alive, she thought, as Melissa dipped her head and fastened her red lips around each of Cherry's reddening nipples in turn.

Each careful nip from Melissa's straight white teeth felt like a cupid's arrow aimed straight for the centre of Cherry's heart, until she could take no more and clutched at Melissa's head, guiding her lover's mouth where she wanted it most. Down, down, down. Melissa kissed a burning path across Cherry's trembling body, past her navel towards the edge of her pubis, until soon she was kneeling on the floor between Cherry's legs. She poked out her tongue lasciviously and touched its wet tip to Cherry's trembling thigh.

'Do you want this?' she asked.

Cherry nodded her assent immediately and planted her legs slightly further apart. A woman's tongue on her clitoris? The thought and the physical sensation combined were like sexual Semtex to Cherry, and her clitoris was the fuse.

Melissa kneaded Cherry's buttocks as she lapped her expert tongue around the ever-hardening centre of Cherry's pleasure. She took her cue from Cherry's breathing. As her excited breaths grew faster, in time with her thudding heart, so did Melissa's tongue, until finally Cherry was gasping for air and the other girl's tongue was moving quicker than a strobe light across Cherry's flesh.

'Don't stop! Don't stop!' said Cherry as her legs began to shake with the anticipation of a climax she had never imagined she would allow herself to have with another girl. She thrashed her head from side to side against the red wall. Her breath escaped from her open mouth in shorter and shorter gasps, punctuated by cries for release that she didn't really want. Not just yet.

'Oh no, oh no.'

Cherry felt as though she was drowning. Falling. She grasped Melissa by the shoulders and held the girl's face hard against her pelvis as the first waves of orgasm began to build inside her. Stars danced behind her flickering eyelids. The sound of the hot blood rushing around her head filled her ears like the roar of an angry sea.

'Aaaaah,' Cherry's grip on Melissa tightened as the sensations exploded deep within her, flooding her limbs with pins and needles, and racing from one extreme of Cherry's body to another, leaving her shuddering, moaning and shaking in its wake like a tiny ship tossed on the sea. Finally her grip on Melissa relaxed and Cherry slumped backwards against the wall. Finished. Exhausted. But ultimately satisfied.

Her knees buckled and she slid down the wall to sit on the cold floor beside Melissa. She let her head drop on to Melissa's shoulder. In the guttering light of the torch, deep red finger marks already showed where Cherry had been gripping so hard. When she looked up again, she caught sight of the other occupants of the room who, having found their own climaxes, had been watching Cherry achieve hers.

Instinctively, Cherry put her hands up to her hot cheeks in embarrassment. But no one could see how red they were in the soft torch-lit darkness of the glittering room. The man and woman on the bed just smiled and shared another complicit glance before he went down on her to return the favour she had just bestowed.

Melissa stroked her cool hand across Cherry's jaw affectionately.

'Beautiful,' she murmured. 'You're beautiful.' Then, gathering up her diaphanous scarf, Melissa floated out of the room without another word. Cherry tried to follow her, but by the time she had found her own flimsy scarf and wrapped it clumsily around her body, she was already two rooms behind her fleet-footed guide.

'Where has she gone?' Cherry turned to ask the lovers on the bed, but they too had disappeared in the time that it took Cherry to turn towards them. In their place, a thick-bodied snake as long as Cherry was tall was coiled upon a pillow. Sensing her in the room, the snake raised its head and flicked out a lazy tongue to taste the air.

Stumbling into the light, Cherry found herself in a room with four doors. She opened them one after another, but found only identical rooms unfolding like the secret compartments of a gigantic magic box. Each room was decorated in exactly the same way – white marble walls were studded with intricate flowers and beautiful wild animals carved from semi-precious stones – so that she couldn't be sure if she had been in any one room before.

She felt another frisson of concern as she looked about her in confusion. From her left came the high, light sound of tinkling female laughter. Or was it from the right? She wasn't sure. Another squeal of pleasure beckoned her into a dead end. The white walls bounced echoes all around.

Cherry struck out in the direction that seemed most likely, but soon found herself back in the room where she had started. Impossible, she told herself, going out through another door and finding herself on the same spot yet again. The laughter still taunted her from some hidden corner, but as fast as she moved towards the source of the sound, the laughing girl seemed to move away.

Doors quite simply disappeared as Cherry drew near them, and where solid walls had once stood between her and her laughing quarry, a window would just as suddenly appear. The laughter rang out again and again. This time Cherry was certain that it came from somewhere far behind her. The unfamiliar sandals on her feet slid on the cold marble floor as she gave pursuit down a corridor that hadn't existed the last time she passed by. When Cherry reached the door she was sure was the last barrier between them, she glanced around to discover to her horror that the wall had crept up behind her.

'Through here!' someone called her.

Cherry fled through another door but still found herself alone.

Where was her guide? Where were the girls who had been teasing the unfortunate man who found himself tied to their pole?

'Where am I?' she shouted.

As though she had been whirled around in a game of blind man's buff, Cherry came out of a giddy spin to find herself at last in the courtyard where the chase had begun. But none of the beautiful revellers she had met before was anywhere to be seen. A single peacock feather lay discarded by the side of a shallow pool. Cherry sat down on the edge and unstrapped her sandals. With her feet dangling in the cool water, supernaturally blue with the reflection of the lapis tiles, Cherry looked about her in the hope of some clue.

Feeling strangely calm, she picked up the feather and dragged it lazily across her naked thighs as she listened. For a while she could hear nothing but the calls of those strange birds, the occasional ear-splitting screech of a peacock as he strutted haughtily across the courtyard in search of a mate. But then Cherry heard a female voice drift across the heavy, warm air towards her and the chase began again. High and wavering, the voice traced out an unfamiliar song that spoke to her clearly of unconditional love and unlimited passion. Cherry turned her head in the direction of the sound, a high tower above the courtyard with elaborately carved columns supporting its tented roof.

Without hesitation, Cherry followed the sound of the voice. She found a doorway at the bottom of the tower and hurried up the narrow winding staircase within to reach the singer.

'Melissa?' she called.

Each time she thought she was nearing the top, another flight of stairs would materialise before her.

'Melissa!'

No answer.

The stairs appeared before her as quickly as she

could climb them. Up and up and up. When Cherry paused to look out of a window, she couldn't see the courtyard below for clouds.

'I can't go up any further,' she panicked.

Then suddenly she was at the top, disbelieving, and catching her breath as she leaned against the doorframe of a room that contained no bed but a vast mound of multicoloured cushions, big enough for a woman of her size to curl up on. In fact, a woman with a fine, firm body that suggested she was only just in her twenties, was doing exactly that. She was curled up like a cat on an orange cushion, watching as a young man with a scarf tied around his eyes to blind him entertained two other women simultaneously.

One of the girls, with a swathe of long auburn hair that swished behind her like a horse's tail, had impaled herself on the man's penis and was riding him furiously, while the other girl, with her full breasts almost completely covered by elaborate gold and silver chains, sat across the man's face and moaned loudly and ecstatically as he massaged her clitoris with his big pink tongue. The woman in the chains massaged the other girl's round breasts and received the same favour in return, completing a very interesting triangle of pleasure. A daisy chain of lust in fact. Cherry smiled.

Soon, the girl who had been watching the proceedings from the orange pillow noticed that she was not the only voyeur. She turned her delicate oval face in Cherry's direction, flashing a meaningful glance from behind the fine white scarf that covered her mouth. Then she stretched her young body to full length, arching her back over the cushion to show herself off to her best advantage. Cherry cast an appreciative glance over the girl's long brown legs, her neatly trimmed pubic hair (almost the shape of a love-heart), and her high, firm breasts with their pink-tipped nipples. But Cherry couldn't be tempted to stay and play. She wanted to find her guide. The girl reached out to grasp Cherry's ankle, only to dissolve into a haze of pink-tinged mist as their bodies made fleeting contact.

In a second, the other lovers were also gone.

Cherry hurried back down the marble staircase to the courtyard, following what she hoped was the sound of Melissa's laugh. As she whirled down the stairs, other men and women were steadily making their way up. Cherry found herself momentarily locked in an embrace with a man who wore nothing but a chain around his waist that emphasised the firm lines of his abdominal muscles.

The stranger pressed his thick hot lips hard into the hollow between Cherry's neck and shoulder. She felt the glistening wet tip of his penis press against the curve below her belly button before he let her go, whispering in her ear 'later' as she drifted on in search of something different.

Cherry found herself in the courtyard once more. She thought she recognised the door to the room in which she had been made love to so expertly, and also the door to the street outside the palace. There was only one further possibility. Cherry turned the handle.

This door led to a further corridor. She took off her sandals again so that she could cover more ground without slipping on the polished marble floor. Archway after archway led to other corridors guarded by endless ranks of columns like soldiers. Cherry could see no one, and yet the sound of laughter seemed to drift out at her from everywhere, mocking her and driving her on.

Suddenly, some way ahead, Cherry thought that she saw the flick of a tail disappearing around a corner; just like the cat in the town house disappearing into the basement. Instantly making the connection in her dream, Cherry raced after the signal and found herself skidding to a halt in a room identical to the one in which she had first seen the pictures. They were all there. The man tied to the trunk while Melissa and her friends stroked him into submission. The girl bending backwards over the stool. The goat-boy fucking her. The hermaphrodite . . .

'Best of both worlds,' murmured someone standing behind her.

She spun around to find herself facing the man who had been tethered to the trunk in the courtyard not so long before. Red welts on the smooth expanse of his chest bore witness to his punishment. He placed his hands on Cherry's cheeks and brought his mouth towards hers for a kiss. Compared to Melissa's butterfly soft caresses, the prisoner's hungry kiss left her feeling engulfed by its forcefulness. The stubble on his square chin scratched at Cherry's downy cheeks. His tongue, so much bigger and thicker than Melissa's, filled her mouth completely.

'You've found our secret lair,' he told her when he

let go, then he led her by the hand across the room to the vast low bed covered in sumptuous silks and fur throws. The exact same bed upon which the black cat had lain in the real world. And there was the little box, too. The prisoner picked it up and placed it out of harm's way.

From out of the shadows stepped another man. Though he was naked, the coronet of gilded laurel on his blond head and the fine gold bracelets that encircled his considerable biceps proclaimed this man as a prince.

'We've been waiting for you,' he assured Cherry, sitting down on the low bed and patting a space beside him. Cherry took her place on the bed between the prisoner and the prince.

'Beautiful, aren't they?' the prince said, as he cast his arm about the room. 'The paintings.'

'They're wonderful,' Cherry agreed.

'They're magnificent. It makes me feel full of lust just to look at them,' he told her, and when she looked down she saw that he did indeed have a hard-on to prove it. A fine golden string encircled the base of the engorged shaft. Cherry had never seen such a thing before, and was staring hard at the place where the string seemed to cut cruelly into the man's pulsating cock when the prisoner took her hand and wrapped it around the very place she had been gazing at.

Cherry was momentarily taken aback that the prisoner seemed to feel so free to manipulate both her own and his superior's body, but when she looked into the prince's glittering eyes, she saw that he was clearly only too happy to be manipulated.

'What do you want me to do?' she asked them nervously.

'Whatever you want to do to us,' the two men answered simultaneously.

Though they were obviously of very different rank in the hierarchy of this peculiar dream palace, the two men were strangely similar. Their bodies were mirror images of each other's. Where the prince's cock curved very slightly to the right at its glistening tip, the prisoner's curved to the left. Their flat stomachs, their strong thighs well defined from running or hunting, corresponded in their symmetry. Like celestial twins. One black. One white.

Cherry tried to swallow her apprehension as the men curled their long legs around hers and encouraged her to lie down. If her experiences with Melissa had been novel, then the situation in which she found herself now was no more familiar. In the heady gloom of an ersatz temple to lust she found herself looking quickly between a prisoner and a prince, one penis in each of her hot and trembling hands. Two pairs of lips were waiting to kiss hers. Two pairs of hands were creeping up her naked thighs, eagerly stroking her quivering breasts, seeking out her hot vagina. Unable to wait any longer, the prisoner pressed a kiss to her bare right shoulder. The prince pressed a kiss to her left. Cherry involuntarily squeezed their two shafts a little harder and elicited an excited and identical sigh from the mouths of her two companions.

'Will you stay with us for just a little while?' the prince asked.

Cherry nodded. Of course she would.

Closing her eyes to better concentrate on her task, she sat up on the bed and began to masturbate both men. It was difficult to keep a rhythm as each bestowed her with kisses and caresses simultaneously. A kiss to one of her tender nipples would make her tug just a little harder. A nip to the side of her neck would make her forget what she was doing and pause for slightly too long.

But they came at exactly the same time. Cherry felt both penises harden in her hands, felt them swell momentarily against her palms, and then they both spasmed violently and urgently as they pushed out jets of sperm that glittered in the air like silver ribbons before they splattered down on to Cherry's naked golden body. Surprising even herself, Cherry let go of their shafts and rubbed the pearly semen across her chest, much to the delight of the two men.

'Your turn now,' the prisoner said.

The prince gave her a little shove and Cherry tumbled on to her back delightedly. The prisoner pulled her legs apart just a little roughly. The prince positioned himself behind Cherry's head, then lifted it on to his sticky lap and held her arms so that she couldn't move while his companion set to work below.

Cherry squirmed with joy as the prisoner took her clitoris into his wide mouth and sucked it into hardness. When it was hard enough, the prisoner used his tongue to flick it gently from side to side. The sensation was exquisite. Cherry arched her back and twisted her narrow wrists in the prince's hands as she tried to escape the intensity of the feelings engulfing her.

When she tried to cry out in pleasure, the prince silenced her with a kiss. Like Melissa, he took just the bow of her top lip into his mouth, sucking hard until Cherry felt that secret pathway Melissa had spoken of open up again. Her clitoris throbbed more intently as energy flooded into it from both external and internal sources now. Her engorged labia pulsated simultaneously, making Cherry want to beg for one of them to enter her with a hotly satisfying shaft.

Pinioning Cherry's arms beneath his knees, the prince transferred his attentions to her rosy nipples. With his mouth on her breasts, Cherry could cry out again. She pleaded to be taken absolutely but her companions refused to oblige her.

The frustration was incredible. It didn't seem possible that they could hold her on the edge of an orgasm for so long. Her body was trembling so much that she was certain she would shake herself apart before she came. The constant pressure of the prisoner's tongue on her clitoris kept her at the peak and yet at the same time she couldn't seem to come. She felt as though she were standing on the very edge of a high cliff, leaning forwards dangerously, expecting to be swept away at any moment. But the strength of the dangerous wind gusting in from the sea was keeping her from going into free-fall just as equally it could be her downfall. It was agonising.

The prince sucked Cherry's nipples harder as the prisoner flicked at her clitoris so quickly it didn't seem humanly possible. Her body arched as the flow of energy reached the point when it could be held back no longer. Her hips bucked upwards violently as her orgasm finally exploded into being. She cried out loud as she shuddered with the energy that those two men had forced into her with their tongues.

It seemed as though Cherry's orgasm would be endless. Even after both men had released her and sat back to watch her shuddering with impassive smiles upon their faces, she jerked and shivered as though their mouths were still upon her. She could feel their breath upon her electrified skin, could taste their salty sweat on her tongue.

Eventually, still giddy with pleasure, Cherry rose unsteadily to her feet and told her lovers that she would be back. At the moment, however, she needed to feel the cold marble of the hallway against her feet. She planned to lie down upon the floor and let the coolness of the snowy stone seep through the whole of her body. With that goal in mind, Cherry stumbled to the doorway and pushed it open with her shoulder.

She expected to find another room beyond the painted chamber, a room that led to another room, *ad infinitum* like before. But this time, when she stepped through her chosen doorway she found herself not in a hallway at all, but right outside the walls of the palace on the dusty road that wound up into the mountains or down towards the sea. Realising her mistake, Cherry whirled round as quickly as she could to catch the door before it slammed shut behind her. But she was too late.

And not only was the door to the palace closed . . . the palace had gone.

She stared in disbelief at the place where it had been only moments before. Where white marble walls lovingly carved by master craftsmen had reached for the soft blue sky, now only a grove of scrubby olive trees wreathed in a strange pink mist stretched their spindly branches upwards. Cherry rubbed her eyes, as if that would make the palace reappear, but when she reopened them she could see only that the trees had clearly been growing in that same spot for tens or even hundreds of years. It was the palace that had been a figment of her imagination.

Suddenly feeling very cold, Cherry began to walk slowly down the dusty red pathway with her flimsy scarf wrapped tightly around her. She wasn't sure where she was going, but instinct told her to head towards the sea. She had walked perhaps ten feet when she found a peacock feather lying across her path. Picking it up, she stroked its tip gently across her cheek and looked wistfully behind her. Still nothing. Only trees. She kept on walking.

Cherry slept right through her alarm. She was still walking down that dry, red path through the Roman countryside, still searching for her Sapphic guide and the mysterious marble palace, when the Wallace and Gromit alarm clock tried to start her day in that particularly irritating way.

When she finally woke naturally, the clock read eight-thirty. Cherry sat up so fast that she almost knocked herself out on the reading lamp she had attached to the headboard in a not so brilliant flash of inspiration. She had meant to be awake by seven. How had she managed to sleep through her alarm again?

For a moment, being late for work was the only thought that filled Cherry's mind, but then, as she groped about on the floor for yesterday's underwear and realised that she couldn't find all of it, the memories of the night before flooded back in glorious technicolor to join forces with a crashing hangover.

'My God,' Cherry murmured, like a coma patient coming round from a two-year slumber, when a vision of the model in the leaf-shaped golden thong flashed before her eyes.

She wasn't sure whether she felt proud or embarrassed as she discovered the faintest of love bites on her breast as she showered. Reaching down to soap between her legs she couldn't help but compare the feeling of a flannel on her clitoris with the feel of a lover's tongue.

By the time she had finished her shower, she was grinning from ear to ear as the picture of the most unusual night of her life so far took on more and more detail. She remembered the strange white house. The hidden room. The erotic paintings. The magic box. The dreams.

Two men! In her dream she had pleasured two men simultaneously. Suddenly the memory of that scene was so vivid that Cherry blushed as if she had really taken two men in her hands and masturbated them to ecstasy.

She was glad that there was no one in the flat but her goldfish to see her grow crimson as she remembered the woman who had also pleasured her in the kingdom of her sleep. She put her hand to her throat as the heat of her blush spread down her neck. If asked, she would have said that she wasn't really attracted to other women, but she was shocked to discover that her first Sapphic encounter with that beautiful girl, however unreal, was the most vivid memory of all.

'The stories you could tell,' Cherry said, dropping a few flakes of fish food into Goldie's bowl before leaving the house at a gallop.

Far more important were the stories that Cherry would have to tell as she rolled up late yet again; 'having a fabulously erotic dream' probably wasn't going to cut the mustard.

# Chapter Four

*WHEN CHERRY FINALLY* arrived at the cool marble-floored offices of the *Daily Mercury*, that morning's editorial meeting for the staff of the *Star Times* was already in full swing.

The lift door opened directly opposite the editor's trendy glass-walled office and Cherry could see all her colleagues sitting at the round table that was meant to make them feel like equals, though in fact there was still a strict hierarchy about who sat nearest to the editor, Eddie Bennett. Cherry froze when the lift door swooshed back, as if staying very still might make her invisible. She had been warned more than once that if she was late for another editorial meeting she might find her precious column had been given to the work experience boy – at present, a rather nice journalism student called Steve.

A thousand options raced through Cherry's mind as she hesitated in the lift. Eddie was standing at the far side of his office, scribbling something on to a white board with a fat black pen. Probably, 'give Cherry's column to Steve', she thought miserably

– but there was a slim possibility that he hadn't yet seen her. Cherry contemplated pressing the down button and racing home again before anyone noticed that she had arrived late. She could call in later with the flu, or pneumonia, or maybe even sudden death. But Cherry had already been noticed.

Steve – who was sitting next to the empty chair usually occupied by Eddie, Cherry noted with a mixture of surprise and disgust – gave her a slow wink. Bastard, she thought. The little work experience creep was clearly one step closer to a staff job. She pressed herself up against the back of the lift wall like a lizard hiding from a bird of prey, and reached out to press the down button with the toe of her stiletto-heeled shoe. But it was too late. Eddie was already opening his office door to greet her.

'Good afternoon, Miss Valentine,' he boomed. Behind him, the sycophants in his office (which meant just about everybody except Karen, the staunchly feminist 'wimmin's' editor, who didn't find anything funny except castration) exploded with laughter. 'So glad you were able to cut your lunch break short to join us.'

'I . . . I . . .' Cherry finally stepped out of the lift, mumbling her excuses as she crept towards Eddie Bennett like a chastened puppy.

'You don't have to explain,' he said jovially. Cherry waited for the rest of the sentence, which should have been, 'Because your P45 is already on the front desk.' But it didn't come. Instead, he said, 'Because Steve here has already told us that you were up all night following a new Madonna story. I sent that roll of film you couriered in straight down to the lab first thing and I have to say – and you know that I don't pay compliments lightly to any of you bunch of reprobates – that I think you may have pulled off the biggest scoop so far this year, Miss Valentine. Even if it is only February.'

Cherry opened and closed her mouth but couldn't find a single word to say to him. Was he taking the piss? What Madonna story? Biggest scoop of the year? Cherry hadn't even managed to fetch herself a scoop of vanilla ice-cream since joining the staff of the *Star Times*. Looking down at her handbag, she noticed that her fists were clenched so tightly around the hard leather handle that she could clearly see her knuckle bones. She concentrated on them in an attempt to stop her knees from shaking. Cherry wasn't scared of many things but she was scared of Eddie Bennett and she was terrified of losing her job while she still had to pay off the loan she had taken out to buy the stupid designer handbag in the first place.

'Don't you want to see how the pictures turned out?' Eddie asked her, sliding an unmarked brown file across the table in her direction. 'Open it up. I think you'll be nearly as chuffed as I am.'

Cherry flipped open the file with a mixture of despair and trepidation, fully expecting to discover her marching orders within. Instead, she actually found some pictures of Madonna. More importantly, some pictures of Madonna on her doorstep sharing a very passionate kiss with a muscle-bound man. The man was wearing nothing but a white vest over his jeans, despite the frosty weather, and had clearly just vacated the legendary singing star's bed.

'Now if I'm not mistaken, I think that young man may already be married to one of this country's brightest stars of stage and screen,' Eddie chortled, holding one of the pictures upside down and peering at it closely. 'Won't our lovely Annie be pleased to see these pics tomorrow morning?'

The Annie in question was Annie Webster. She was Britain's biggest new actress, having sky-rocketed to fame in a big-budget action pic about alien landings in which she played a nuclear scientist to Leonardo DiCaprio's uneducated but naturally brilliant bowling alley attendant. The *Star Times* had championed her until she got an Oscar nomination. Now Eddie seemed determined to chip the poor girl back down to size.

'How do you want your name under the pictures?' Eddie asked her. 'Or do you perhaps not want your name associated with this filth at all? Another couple of stars to add to your list of ex-best friends, eh? Don't think you'll be going to Madonna's birthday party this year.'

'Yeah,' murmured Cherry, sinking into a chair. To her amazement, it was becoming clear that Eddie really did believe she had taken those pictures. She spent the rest of the meeting scouring the faces of the other members of the team to find out who really was responsible for the amazing photos, but nobody was giving anything away. Sandy was still trying to persuade Eddie to send him to cover some story on drug smuggling in the Caribbean. Marsha was plugging her 'women who have given up sex' idea for an interesting 'real-life' article (the point being that she had recently given up having sex with Eddie and wanted to explain exactly why in humiliating detail).

When the meeting finally ended, Eddie came up behind Cherry and gave her such a hearty pat on her shoulder that she almost fell over under its force. 'I knew you could do it, Cherry,' he told her. 'When I took you on, against a lot of opposition from my superiors I have to say, I said to myself, there is a girl with a nose for the news. A real newshound. Not to say that you're a dog, of course, my darling.'

'Of course,' said Cherry.

'And if I've been a little hard on you lately, I just want you to know that it's nothing personal,' Eddie continued. 'I've been a bit on edge since I gave up smoking. Got this hypnotism tape now though.' He took the tape box from his top pocket to show her. 'So I reckon I'll have kicked the weed and be back to my normal self before too long.'

Cherry nodded sceptically. The tape was called 'Quit Smoking Instantly' by none other than Andreas Eros. Cherry wondered what qualified the jumped-up jokester to pretend that he could change a stranger's habits of a lifetime with his mellifluous voice. But she didn't say that to Eddie. Instead, before he could elaborate, she told him, 'I've got to get down to the clippings library and do some research around this great story.'

'You do that,' Eddie said, with another hearty slap.

Cherry found herself a quiet corner of the clippings library, where news stories were filed in bundles according to subject. She made a pillow of her cardigan and handbag with the intention of catching up on some sleep.

She also wanted to do some thinking about the previous night. Strangely, it seemed as though the more she tried to remember her experiences now, the less came back, and that was starting to worry her. Perhaps it was because she suddenly felt so tired. She was just nodding off with her head on a pile of old pictures of Jack Nicholson when Steve slipped into the chair beside her.

'Hi,' he said shyly.

'Hi,' Cherry muttered. 'You woke me up.'

'I don't blame you for trying to catch up on some kip. Sounds like you had a hard night last night. Chasing the Madonna story, eh? How did you know she'd be at her flat in Cadogan Gardens? I thought she was supposed to be filming her new movie in LA.'

'Little bird told me,' Cherry said flatly, hoping that he wasn't going to expect any gory details.

'Well, you had better let that same little bird tell you that those pictures weren't taken at Cadogan Gardens at all. I think you'll find they were snapped outside a recently renovated house in Holland Park.'

Cherry forced herself to sit upright, and she stared at him in disbelief.

'So it was you who took those pictures?' she said, quickly adding up the evidence.

Steve gave her a little closed-lipped smile and a modest nod.

'What? When? Why?' Cherry mouthed.

'When I came in this morning, Eddie was spouting off to Sandy that if you weren't in the office by nine o'clock, Sandy could have your column. But I don't fancy Sandy . . .'

Cherry smiled at that. 'So you let Eddie think that I was out stalking Madonna to save my arse and gave him your pictures as proof?'

Steve nodded again.

'Oh, Steve. What were you thinking of?' Cherry sighed, though she was secretly mightily relieved. She hadn't even considered that Steve might have been the photographer, expecting instead to find that it was someone more experienced who would be after her for a big favour shortly afterwards. Blackmail was common currency at the *Star Times*. Steve was too nice for that though. Wasn't he?

'So what do you want?' Cherry asked cautiously.

'Nothing,' he replied.

Cherry couldn't quite believe that. 'But those photos were incredible. They're worth a fortune in syndication fees. You could have sold them to anybody. You could have made your name.'

'And you could have lost your job without them. You're the best writer on this paper, Cherry. Sandy can't even spell his own name.'

'You don't need to butter me up,' Cherry grinned, though nothing cheered her up quite as much as hearing that someone else had noticed Sandy's basic inability to grasp the rules of the English language. 'But thanks all the same. I guess I must owe you lunch for this.'

'That'd be nice.'

'Shall we go now?' Cherry asked him.

'What? It's only ten-thirty in the morning,' Steve protested in surprise.

'So? I need to follow up that Madonna lead while she's still in town and I need you to help me carry my camera...'

Steve looked at her disapprovingly.

'OK, so that's not entirely the truth,' Cherry admitted. 'But I have got to get out of here right now, whatever the excuse. My head is killing me and my mouth feels like a camel's arse.'

'Big night?' Steve asked her.

'You could say that.'

'Fancy a hair of the dog?'

'Too right. The whole bloody coat of it in fact. As soon as the Dog and Duck opens.'

By eleven o'clock, Cherry and Steve were sitting in the sad-looking bar of the Dog and Duck in Soho with a handful of other hardened drinkers who had been leaning on the door when the barman took the latch off.

Cherry had chosen a nice dark corner and let Steve sit in the little light that could get through the dirty windows. He was young, he could take the illumination. As she thought this, Cherry realised that she wasn't sure how old he actually was, but he was probably only in his early twenties, at least eight years younger than herself. Young enough to throw away the biggest chance of his career through his misguided naive altruism. She knew that he had only recently finished some college course.

'So what were you doing last night?' Steve asked her jovially.

'Just because you did me a huge favour doesn't

mean you can ask such personal questions,' said Cherry in a warning tone.

'Sorry.'

'No, it's OK. I shouldn't be so rude to someone who's done me such a big service. I was following up a lead of my own, actually. But unfortunately, I don't think anything is going to come of it. It was a bit of a funny night,' she added, knitting her brows together as she remembered more of the sordid detail. Or at least, thought she remembered something.

'Want to discuss it?'

'No,' said Cherry quickly. 'There isn't much to discuss. Not yet.'

In fact, as she sobered up in the cold light of a London morning Cherry was beginning to wonder if there was anything to discuss at all. Could she possibly have dreamed the whole thing? She knew that she had dreamed up the orgy in ancient Rome, but perhaps she had dreamed the house in Belgravia that inspired her too. She certainly didn't think she would really have lain down on a stranger's bed and masturbated had she been properly awake!

What if someone had slipped her something hallucinogenic at the Promised Pleasures party? It was possible. She read about such things happening all the time. And that train of thought led smoothly and logically on to the distinct and utterly disturbing possibility that rather than having been made love to in her dreams by all those gorgeous different people, she had in fact been making love in very real life to that fat old hack who called himself 'Melissa' for his column.

She shuddered visibly.

'You OK?' Steve asked, putting his hand gently on her knee.

'Just the hangover. I honestly don't know why I drink at all any more. It's not worth the pain the next morning. Look, take my mind off it will you Steve? Why don't you tell me about yourself? Tell me your life story. What made you want to get your hands grubby with newsprint for the rest of your life?'

'It seemed like the most exciting career I could get into after taking an English degree,' he began idealistically, before launching into a long spiel about his journalistic idols and mentors that soon had Cherry slipping into a trance. His voice was just so soft and soothing. And she still felt so tired. She could only keep her eyes open by forcing herself to make a detailed observation of his face.

His eyes, she noticed first, wide open with youthful enthusiasm, were the same blue as the soft denim fabric of the shirt he was wearing. His mouth was unusually full and smooth for a man's. When he turned sideways to see if anyone he knew was in the bar before he imparted some piece of particularly scurrilous gossip, Cherry couldn't help thinking that in profile Steve looked like a carving of a young Egyptian king, with his long straight nose and those fine, high cheekbones. His fair hair was cropped close to his head and Cherry had a sudden urge to reach out her hand and stroke the fuzzy surface of his perfectly rounded skull. He really was quite ridiculously attractive and she wondered why she had never noticed as much before.

Not only was his face pretty amazing, his body

was astonishingly well proportioned too. Cherry allowed her eyes to slip down over his broad chest as he told her about his busy year at journalism college. By the time he got round to telling her about his prized work placement on *The Times*, she was just letting her gaze wander across his crotch from one well-muscled thigh to the other before finally bringing her eyes to rest on the haven of his button fly.

'Are you feeling OK, Cherry?' he asked her suddenly. 'Only your head seems to be drooping. I thought you were falling asleep back there.'

Cherry jerked her eyes up again to meet his baby blues.

'I am feeling a bit weird,' she admitted, embarrassed that he had almost caught her perving.

Weird? That was an understatement. What was she doing? Lusting after Steve the work experience lad? That was ridiculous. Cherry put the blame on her hormones. It would go some way to explaining why she had jumped on that model at the Promised Pleasures party, and had those crazy dreams as well. All morning she had been feeling strangely aware of her body. The cold wall at the back of the elevator as she leaned on it on the way up to the office; the draught drifting across Eddie's room as he congratulated her on the Madonna photos; even the feel of the worn velvet on the pub stool beneath her fingers as she struggled to sit up and pay attention. All these things had aroused something more in her than the usual rash of goosebumps that day. She felt hypersensitive, as if her hearing, her sense of smell, her sense of touch, had all been cranked up a gear. When

Steve leaned across the brass-topped table to light her cigarette from his Zippo, the smell of his aftershave sent a shiver down her back like water dripping from an icicle.

It was a frisson she hadn't felt since ... well, since Aaron had agreed to help her find her clitoris, she had to admit.

'Perhaps I ought to go back to my flat and have a kip before we go back to the office,' she told Steve suddenly, thinking that she had better stay out of trouble, and that flirting with work colleagues was one of the quickest routes to trouble she knew.

'Do you want me to come with you?' he asked.

'What?' Cherry spluttered out a mouthful of lager.

'Do you want me to come with you? Only it might look a little odd if I go back to the office on my own right now, don't you think? Considering that I'm supposed to be helping you with the Madonna story today.'

Cherry's face relaxed into another grin. 'I see. For a minute there, I thought you might be propositioning me.'

'Would you be offended if I was?' he smiled.

Would she hell? Any good intentions still knocking around in Cherry's feeble conscience regarding Steve's innocence were trampled in the rush to the pub door. Cherry ordered a cab back to her flat and less than half an hour later she was finding out firsthand whether Steve's body was as good as she had imagined it would be under that sky-blue shirt.

If he had been joking about propositioning her while they chatted in the pub, he soon took the idea more seriously. Cherry had placed an exploratory hand on his knee as they sat in traffic in the taxi. She figured that if he was offended, she could pretend that she had merely wanted to draw his attention to the display in some shop window they were passing. When he didn't ask her to move it or try to shrug it off, she gave him a little squeeze. Then his hand crept on to her thigh and by the time she had paid off the driver and got her key into the front door of her building, Steve was kissing the back of her neck.

Once inside, Steve shuddered with pleasure as Cherry peeled his denim shirt from his broad shoulders and cast it to the corner of the room like a silk handkerchief. She wasn't disappointed with what she found beneath. With his clothes off, Steve was exactly as she had imagined. His wide, brown chest, smattered with just the lightest trace of curling hair, glistened in the little light that managed to squeeze through the blinds Cherry had so hurriedly closed.

'Wow,' she breathed.

Steve pulled her against him and enfolded her in bear-like arms.

'You feel like you work out,' she told him as she ran her hands eagerly over the bulging muscles in his back.

'Not really,' he replied.

'So you're naturally like this? Don't make me jealous,' she warned him.

'Why should you be jealous?' he asked. 'You've got a beautiful body too. The most beautiful body.' He let his hands follow the curve of her waist over the clinging jersey of her simple black dress. Cherry arched her back and reached up to untie her black hair from its messy little pony-tail.

When she had finished, Steve raked his hands through her loosened bob and stared at her intently. He licked his lips as he prepared to say something difficult.

'What is it?' she asked.

'Ever since I started at the paper I've had fantasies about you, Cherry,' he murmured. 'I can remember the first time I saw you. You walked into Eddie's office to bawl him out about sending Sandy to interview Elton John instead of you because you were just ten minutes late getting into the office that morning. You were wearing this dress, in fact.' He smoothed his hands over her breasts. 'I couldn't take my eyes off you. You're gorgeous.'

'Keep going,' said Cherry as Steve slid his hand beneath the hem of her dress and started to make his way steadily up her shapely stockinged leg.

'The first thing I noticed about you was that you walked like a woman who knew the power of her body,' he continued. 'In fact, you don't just walk. You sway. You glide. When you crossed the floor of the office, you looked like a model sashaying down a catwalk. And then, when you stopped at Eddie's desk and leaned across it to shout into his face, your anger was so erotic. I was standing right beside him. Do you remember? I tried to imagine that you were talking to me. I had a front row view right down your v-neck to your orange satin bra.'

'That's my favourite bra,' she told him.

Cherry shivered pleasurably as Steve pulled the neckline of her dress open now and gazed lasciviously at her naked breasts beneath. She hadn't been able to find any sort of bra in her hurry to get to work that morning. Never mind.

'All I wanted to do was reach inside that slinky dress and take both your breasts in my hands,' Steve continued. 'I wanted to feel their warm weight in my palms. I wanted to squeeze them gently. Stroke them. I wanted to take that amazing bra off and sink my teeth into your hardened nipples.'

Cherry sighed. Steve was rolling one of her nipples between his fingers now. To think that he had thought all this on their very first meeting, and yet it had taken Cherry so long to take advantage of his feelings.

She felt absolutely naked under Steve's gaze, though she was still wearing her dress. Like a woman hypnotised, she slowly raised her arms above her head and let him pull it off. She stood before him then in nothing but a pair of ethereally fine hold-up stockings and a g-string. Steve momentarily let her go in order to take the rest of his own clothes off. His hard-on had already broken through his boxer shorts and was poking out from the buttonless fly to greet her when he let his battered jeans drop to the floor.

Cherry couldn't keep her hands off him for a moment longer. She helped him to push his striped shorts down his strongly-muscled legs, then took his beautiful hard-on in her hands and, kneeling before him, put her lips to the strong, pink shaft to bestow a tantalising kiss just as Melissa had done for the captive man in Cherry's dream. Up above her, Steve groaned in pleasure and twisted her black hair in his enthusiasm.

Cherry straightened up again and pressed her semi-naked body fully against his. Steve pounced upon her lips, forcing them apart with his tongue. Kissing as passionately and violently as two tigers fighting, they stumbled backwards towards the door that led to Cherry's bedroom, and tumbled on to the untidy bed that she hadn't made for two days.

Steve pushed the crumpled duvet aside and lay Cherry down on the smooth white sheet that covered the mattress. He climbed on to the bed with her, then sat back on his heels and just stared, as if he were an artist appraising a painting he had just finished. Cherry luxuriated in his steady gaze which told her all that she needed to know right then. Steve's beautiful smooth lips were a deep pink and plump with arousal. His denim blue eyes were almost completely black now as his pupils dilated wide to indicate the strength of his desire for her. He wanted her so much right then that Cherry could almost see his need in the air between them like an American Indian smoke signal.

'You're gorgeous,' he sighed.

He reached for her g-string and traced its shape with fingers that trembled with anticipation. Moments later, he rolled it down over her fine black stockings. Then he leaned forward slowly and nuzzled his nose and chin into the silky dark triangle of pubic hair the g-string had been covering.

With nothing but her stockings on, Cherry looked like a French whore in a painting by Toulouse Lautrec. And she liked it. She liked the sly appreciative smile on Steve's face as he stroked his hands along her silk-covered legs. She liked the feel of his hot breath as he kissed her on the pale skin just above her stocking tops, where her legs felt somehow all the more sensitive for being only partially covered.

'You don't know how many times I've imagined this moment,' Steve murmured, bestowing featherlight kisses on Cherry's breasts which made her nipples pucker and harden even more.

'How many times?' she asked him. 'Tell me.'

She wanted to know more, hear more. She was unspeakably aroused by the thought of all the time he had spent secretly watching her across the busy office. She thought about one particular occasion when she had caught him looking at her legs while she sat on his desk to talk to him about some unspeakably boring article she wanted him to have a go at editing. She hadn't drawn much of a conclusion from it at the time. Men look at legs, don't they? They just do.

But now that innocent moment was imbued with so much more meaning. Cherry closed her eyes and allowed herself a delicious moment of fantasy. Steve was sliding his hand between her legs. In her fantasy, they were back in the office and she was sitting on the edge of his desk. He was sliding his hand between her legs there too. His strong fingers pulled her lacy knickers out of the way and began to massage her clitoris expertly while all the time he continued to talk to her with an impassive look on his face, as if nothing untoward was going on. Meanwhile, the rest of the office staff carried on around them. Laughing. Shouting. They had no idea that Steve was sliding his finger in and out of Cherry's slick vagina as they worked.

'I wish I'd known how you felt,' Cherry told him between gasps, as back in the moment his finger really did slip inside her aching body.

'Would you have acted on it?' he asked her.

'Oh, definitely,' she breathed, arching her back in a spasm of pure joy.

Steve thrust another finger inside her. This time there was no resistance. Cherry was so wet with her desire for him, he could be left in no doubt that she was delighted to have discovered his feelings for her.

Cherry ran her hands feverishly over Steve's soft hair, down along the back of his bare neck and over his muscular shoulders. He fixed her with his summer blue eyes and gazed at her intently. They were silent for a while apart from the sound of their breathing. Occasionally Cherry gasped with surprise as Steve thrust his fingers a little harder and touched some part of her deep inside that caused her to shudder with delight.

Meanwhile, Steve's penis was hardening in readiness. He lay on his side next to Cherry so that it rested lightly on her hip while he brought her closer to the perfect state of bliss. Cherry arched her back again so that his hand thrust deeper inside. She clawed up handfuls of bedding in her sweating palms as she tried not to come too soon.

Glancing down at their entwined bodies, she saw Steve's penis lying across her hip, could feel its welcome damp warmth on her desire-electrified skin. At its tip, a tiny bead of semen glistened invitingly. Cherry felt that she had never wanted anything so much as she wanted Steve's long stiff cock inside her then. All the way inside. She reached down and took his penis in one hand. Rolling herself towards him so that he had to take his fingers out of her, she used her other hand to gently fondle his balls.

They kissed again, this time even more urgently than before. Steve's pointed tongue filled Cherry's mouth in a direct echo of what he wanted to do elsewhere, and soon. Taking her by the shoulders, he rolled her on to her back and climbed on top of her, a look of frightening emotional intensity upon his handsome face. Cherry parted her slender legs automatically and reached between their bodies to help guide him inside.

As Steve slid his hard penis into Cherry's welcoming vagina, they continued to kiss. He took her top lip between both of his, and for just a fleeting second Melissa's smile flitted across her mind. But as soon as Steve pulled his mouth away from hers and made the first proper thrust of their love-making, Cherry was back with him again. Absolutely with him.

He kept his eyes fixed firmly on her as he moved. She could tell by the concentrated look that remained on his handsome face even now he was inside her that he wanted this to be perfect. He wanted so much to please her. And suddenly she wanted to please him too.

She lifted her long legs from the bed and wrapped her thighs tightly around his waist, crossing her feet behind his back to keep steady. Immediately, Steve thrust deeper than before. Each movement filled Cherry so absolutely that she felt almost light-headed as her breath was pushed from her body. She took hold of Steve's buttocks in her eager hands and pulled him even further inside.

When she closed her eyes again, the blood racing around her head made bright psychedelic patterns inside her fluttering eyelids. She felt giddy; faint with a fatal mixture of excitement and lust. She dug her fingers into Steve's shoulders, as if by feeling his skin yield beneath her nails she could make sure that her soul was still inside her body. She felt so wonderfully light-headed that she expected to be able to look down on her body from the ceiling.

'Come with me now,' she begged him as the first clear rumble of her orgasm began.

But Steve wasn't quite ready. Instead, he withdrew his penis, slick and shining with Cherry's juices, and flipped her over on to her front. As she lay there, almost drowning in the pillows, Steve hooked his arm beneath her narrow waist and pulled her up on to all fours. In this new position he took her again. Grabbing her waist with both hands he drove forward and impaled her with his bulging penis.

Cherry yelped with delighted surprise, but quickly settled into this new rhythm. Steve pulled her buttocks back against his body, faster and faster and faster. Cherry could feel her own body begin to hum again as if she were a fine glass and Steve was running a wet finger around her rim to make her sing.

As if she could have been any more aroused right then, Cherry reached back between her own trembling legs and began to fondle her clitoris while Steve thrust on from behind. She knew that she wouldn't be able to hold back for much longer.

'Yes!' Steve shouted as he began to come too. Triumphantly, he pressed his pelvis hard against Cherry as he pumped his orgasm into her body. Cherry meanwhile was in the throes of a rocket-fuelled orgasm of her own. The over-heated muscles inside her vagina clamped tightly around Steve's penis, as if that might draw him further in, and pulsed in time with the spurts of Steve's semen. For a moment, it was as though they were part of the same ethereal organism. Their bodies throbbed in perfect time, shaking, shuddering with the power of their delight, until finally they slowed down simultaneously and Cherry sank back on to the bed, Steve lying heavily on top of her.

They rolled apart, laughing and panting. When Cherry reached across the little stretch of empty bed between their bodies to take Steve's hand, he was already reaching out to take hers.

'We shouldn't have done that,' Cherry told him between giggles.

'I'm glad we did though. How was it for you?' he asked, just a little proudly.

'If you must ask such a cheesy question then I suppose I ought to tell you that it's made me feel like eating a pizza,' said Cherry, punching him playfully in the arm. She picked up the phone with the intention of ordering a big one. 'Good sex always makes me hungry, and right now I'm ravenous.'

'I could give you something less fattening to nibble on,' said Steve. He gently prised the telephone receiver from her hand before climbing astride her and pointing his penis towards her mouth. He was already hard. It didn't take much for him to be ready for action all over again. The main advantage of going for a young man, Cherry thought; what they lacked in expertise they more than made up for in enthusiasm and stamina. Though she had to admit that Steve seemed to have the necessary expertise as well.

'Just a little bite?' asked Steve.

Cherry playfully turned her head away from his glistening helmet.

'Not now. I think we should have a shower and then get some pizza,' she said in her most determined voice.

'I think I can change your mind,' said Steve.

'I'd like to see you try,' said Cherry, rolling out from beneath him. Though in reality, she didn't doubt that he would be able to change her mind with just the tiniest bit more effort.

He followed her eagerly into the bathroom and caressed her buttocks lovingly as she leaned into the shower cubicle to set the water temperature before they got in. When it was warm enough, she stepped inside and dragged Steve after her by the big stiff handle of his dick. Gently, of course.

The shower cubicle in Cherry's pokey bathroom wasn't really big enough for two and it seemed that one or the other of them was always having to lean against the cold tiled wall. The only way to keep warm was to cling to each other under the weedy trickle of water and soon, inevitably, Cherry supposed, they were kissing again.

'Not now, Steve,' she said, pulling away from him half-heartedly. 'We should probably go back to the office before the end of the day.'

Steve pulled a face.

'Just wash me,' said Cherry, kissing him on the end of his nose.

Steve poured a shining dollop of musk-scented shower gel into his hand and began to massage it into a lather on Cherry's smooth wet body. As the foam grew thicker and more luxurious, his hands moved across her skin more quickly. She turned her flushed pink face toward the shower head and let the warm water trickle into her mouth as Steve soaped her breasts. She tried to resist the urge to let Steve have her all over again, but resistance wasn't easy while he was focusing all his concentration on her pleasure.

Cherry's rose-pink nipples were soon almost as hard as Steve's magnificent penis. And when the shower had all but washed the soap suds away, Steve set to kissing each of the delicate pink buds in turn, working his magic with his tongue. It wasn't long before Cherry finally conceded that she wouldn't be going back to the office anytime soon.

She turned the hot tap up until the tiny cubicle was full of steam. As the water vapour billowed up towards her, Cherry couldn't really see Steve clearly but she could certainly feel him, his hands sliding from her shoulders to her waist, then down over her slick, wet hips as he sank to his knees on the roughly tiled floor, designed to prevent nasty accidents. She felt his hands between her legs, encouraging her to set her feet a little further apart. She felt him slip a finger inside her longing vagina, while at the same time he nuzzled the damp triangle of her pubic hair with his perfect nose.

'Still want to go to work?' he asked her as he moved his attention to her clitoris.

'Just keep quiet and keep working here,' Cherry told him.

'You're the boss,' he agreed, simultaneously applying such perfect pressure to her g-spot that it made her want to cry out with delight. He wrapped his free arm around her thighs so that she couldn't move too far away from him, though there was hardly anywhere to escape to in such a tiny space.

Cherry leaned back against the cold tiled wall, which didn't feel quite as icy now that she was so hot, and let Steve do his expert best. It wasn't long before he pulled his fingers from her vagina and set to licking her into a frenzy instead.

At first, the touch of his tongue was so delicate that it was almost ticklish, but then he changed the tempo. Cherry raised one leg and balanced with her foot on the silver taps so that Steve could better reach his target. With careful fingers, he parted her glistening labia and applied long, firm strokes from the very edge of her vagina towards her clitoris until she begged him to stop.

'You want me to stop?' he said quizzically.

'Yes. I mean, no,' she said. 'I just want you to take me again. Properly.'

Quickly cranking the taps shut, Steve wrapped his arms around Cherry and lifted her out of the shower cubicle. Wrapping her in a fluffy white towel, the only towel in the bathroom, he scooped her up again and carried her back to the bedroom. She let herself be carried, enjoying the sensation of being momentarily helpless in his arms.

Once in the room, Steve set her down carefully on the edge of the bed and began to unwrap the towel in which he had covered her as though he were unwrapping an exquisite present. Level with his waist and almost eye to eye with his magnificent shaft, Cherry wrapped her arms around his wet body and covered his taut, toned belly with urgent, gentle kisses.

'I can't get enough of you,' Steve murmured into her wet, tangled hair.

'You can have as much as you want,' she said, moving her kisses down across his abdomen to where his hard-on waited patiently for her attention.

Steve massaged her shoulders as she sucked at his beautiful dick. The taste of shower gel on his shaft couldn't disguise the essential masculinity of his scent, and soon Cherry tasted salt as semen oozed out in preparation to lubricate their love.

Steve sighed half in anguish as he pulled away from her mouth, but right then he needed more than a blow-job. Cherry rolled back on to the bed and let her mouth spread in a wide, wide smile as he climbed on top of her and parted her legs.

Lukewarm water from the shower dripped from Steve's hair on to Cherry's breasts. He licked up the drops, making her nipples pucker a little more with each touch of his tongue. His legs were outside Cherry's as he kneeled over her, but she quickly changed that, bringing her knees up to her chest before straightening her legs on the outside of Steve's muscular thighs. She was ready for him again. She slid her body a little lower on the bed and arched herself up to meet him.

Steve cupped a delicate pink breast in each hand and brought them together, burying his hot mouth in the deep warm valley between them. But Cherry wanted more. She wrapped her legs around his back and tried to pull him down towards her. Sensing her desperation, Steve took hold of his shaft and gently, teasingly, touched its wet, sticky tip to Cherry's clitoris. She squirmed with excitement, and tried to pull him closer.

Steve lowered himself so that his penis stroked the length of Cherry's labia, leaving a slick of semen on her satin lips. Cherry set her legs further apart, braced them against the bed and pushed upwards. But still Steve wouldn't enter her. Cherry felt an urgent quiver of sensation deep inside. She closed her eyes to feel it better. When she opened them again, Steve still held his penis steady just outside her vagina. His eyes were closed too and his mouth stretched wide into an ecstatic smile.

'Take me,' she begged him in a whisper.

She knew that anticipation was often more than half the enjoyment, but right then she really couldn't wait any longer. The thought of Steve's penis inside her filled her mind. She couldn't breathe as she waited for the moment to arrive. Every tiny sensation as the tip bumped against the entrance to her vagina was translated into a massive rush of arousal that made her reply to each minute contact between their bodies with a visible shudder.

'I can't wait any longer,' she begged.

Steve grinned with the knowledge of his power over her desires as he finally edged his way inside her. The wait he had forced her to endure had been so long that Cherry felt as though she would orgasm immediately. She felt her vagina contract around Steve's penis as though taking receipt of a longed-for prize. When their pelvises touched, it was as though they were connecting at a far less tangible level too. Cherry's limbs were weak with excitement. She barely had the strength to wrap her arms around Steve's back as he started to move.

Though she hadn't believed it possible, this time the sex was even better than before. Steve knew her rhythm already and he didn't feel the need to explode so urgently and hurriedly himself. He oozed in and out of her with luxuriating languor. Cherry felt, not for the first time, as though she was being played like some precious stringed instrument, a viola fashioned from rare mahoghany perhaps. Many men would have been afraid to touch her but not Steve. Steve was a virtuoso, he could make the curves of her beautiful body sing for him; deep notes of longing building to a crescendo that would rip through them both.

'Do it harder,' she told him huskily. 'Faster.'

Steve responded to her wishes at once. His beautiful mouth was set in a hard line of determination as he thrust into her powerfully with strokes that hammered against her swollen clitoris and drove her closer to the edge.

Somewhere deep inside, Cherry had the sensation again of standing on the edge of a cliff, leaning forward into the wind, trusting that it would hold her still. Her stomach was in her mouth and she felt almost weightless in the long, slow seconds before her orgasm at last set in.

How quickly it took hold of every nerve in her shaking body. Cherry was coming long before Steve this time. Her body throbbed around the exquisite focus of his penis. Steve continued to thrust, his face smiling down on hers with a mixture of pleasure and pride. Cherry's forehead was furrowed by deep concentration but her mouth echoed his in a mile-wide grin.

'Come with me,' she begged him as joy racked her body. 'Please come with me.'

Her pleadings were answered. Steve found the strength to push himself into her just one more time before his orgasm took hold. Cherry opened her eyes to see him coming. She wanted to savour this experience with all of her senses. She wanted to see his face lose control as his thrusts lost their timing and became uncontrolled, as his come exploded from him into her body, covering the walls of her vagina and making her shudder even harder.

Cherry could feel the powerful spasm of his penis as it shot his sperm deep inside her again and again. She rode Steve's climax, clinging to his body tightly. She didn't want to let go of him ever again. She wanted him to be inside her for ever. She wanted to come with him for ever. She wanted this orgasm to be eternal. To go on and on and on.

Eventually, though, it had to come to an end. Steve rolled off Cherry's body and then pulled her back against his stomach so that they lay like spoons. She closed her tired eyes with Steve's body still curled around hers. Protecting her. Keeping her warm. When she opened her eyes again, the room had grown dark and cold around their entangled bodies. They had been asleep for three hours. It was seven o'clock.

'Oh no,' Cherry groaned. 'It's too late to go back to the office now.'

'Time flies when you're having fun,' murmured Steve as he shook himself awake.

'Too much fun,' said Cherry, who was already on her way to the bathroom with the lone towel clutched to her body. 'This is a disaster. You'll have to ring Eddie and tell him that we're on a stake-out somewhere. He'll kill me. You've got to phone him.'

'Your wish is my command,' Steve assured her sleepily. 'After we've had another shower, though. It'll give us time to make up a convincing story.'

Cherry cranked the shower taps open with a smile. 'You'll have to let me concentrate,' she told him.

'I can't promise that,' he said, pressing his naked body against hers. This time though they actually did manage to get clean without succumbing to the temptation to fall back into bed and get dirty all over again. Much to Steve's disappointment. Cherry promised she would review the situation once she had had some pizza. She was absolutely ravenous now and she didn't think it would be fair to let Steve get to work on her again while all she could think of was mozzarella and pepperoni. That would have been a terrible insult to his very real abilities.

'How long am I going to have to wait?' he asked, pushing her down into the pillows once more so that her wet hair spread out around her head like a halo.

'Be patient,' she told him.

'I can't,' he insisted, covering her cheeks with

little pecking kisses. 'I think you should tell me what you were doing last night to keep me occupied.'

Cherry narrowed her eyes. 'Last night?' she echoed. Being with Steve had gone a long way to taking her mind off the previous night's excitement. She bit her lip as she considered telling him what had happened. He might be able to reassure her that she had been letting her imagination run away with her.

But just then the doorbell rang. Saved from having to reveal what she had been thinking, Cherry leapt up to answer the caller.

'The pizza,' she assured Steve.

But it wasn't the pizza delivery boy. Instead, it was another man in uniform. Smart suit instead of overalls. Peaked cap rather than a helmet. Cherry regarded her unexpected visitor suspiciously through the security spy-hole in her front door. Then she stepped back and rubbed at her sleep-blurred eyes. She hadn't really seen much of his face to recognise him by, but Cherry was sure that the man standing outside her door was the chauffeur who had driven her from the Promised Pleasures party and to that altogether more interesting house. But that simply wasn't possible. Was it?

# Chapter Five

CHERRY OPENED THE door to her visitor cautiously, keeping the safety chain on so that it would be harder for him to force his way in, should he try. After all, there was a serious possibility that the chauffeur had come to drive her straight to the nearest police station for having broken into his employer's house and availed herself of his hospitality uninvited. Or worse.

'What do you want?' she asked curtly.

'I've come to take you back to the white house,' the chauffeur said quietly.

'What?' said Cherry.

'The white house,' he repeated.

It was what she had hoped he would say, and yet it still came as a bit of a shock to hear it. This was it. This was proof that she hadn't imagined the previous night's events. The white house did exist. Therefore the painted room must exist too. They hadn't been a part of her dream.

'I was told to come here and bring you back with me,' the driver continued. 'Your host of yesterday evening is very anxious to see you at his house again.'

'But I didn't meet my host,' Cherry said suspiciously. 'Did I?' She remembered the light she thought she had seen at an upstairs window.

'I am under strict instructions not to return to the house without you,' the chauffeur said, not giving away a thing.

'How did you get my address?' Cherry asked him.

'It was in your purse,' said the chauffeur simply. 'You dropped it in the car last night.'

The chauffeur passed a small leather purse through the gap in the door. It was indeed hers. Cherry opened it. All the money she had taken with her to the Promised Pleasures party – what little there was of it – was still inside, untouched. As was her NUJ membership card. Which very clearly stated her name and occupation. In which case, why had the chauffeur come for her? Why hadn't he sent some heavies round to find out what she knew about the house and make her solemnly promise that their master or mistress would never see it in print?

'Who is it?' Steve called from the bedroom.

The chauffeur tried to look beyond Cherry into the untidy house.

'It's the bailiffs,' Cherry lied as she called back to Steve. 'You stay there. I'll be back in a minute.'

The chauffeur looked at her quizzically from beneath the brim of his hat.

'Plumber,' she said, for his benefit. 'Come to fix the shower.'

The chauffeur looked at Cherry's own still-damp hair dubiously but said nothing.

'I don't understand why your employer wants to see me again,' Cherry whispered.

'Neither do I,' said the chauffeur, slightly disdainfully. 'Perhaps he wants to thank you for having the decency to post his keys through the letterbox. So are you going to come with me or not?' he asked.

She hesitated for a moment. This was utterly bizarre. She had seen no one at the house. She had left her purse in the car, but that gave the chauffeur no reason to suspect that she had actually been inside the house. Thank her for pushing his keys through the letterbox, though? That had to be sarcasm.

Any other woman would have closed the door and demanded that Steve sort out the driver with his fists, but Cherry wasn't an ordinary woman. Her mind had clicked out of the haze brought on by an afternoon of love-making and was back into full-on journalist mode. Perhaps, far from wanting to keep her quiet, this man's employer had discovered Cherry's press card and wanted to make a confession that she could turn into news. It was a long shot. But some of the most successful journalists Cherry knew had made careers on the back of long shots.

Besides which, Cherry was more than a little curious to find out about the origin of the painted cellar. Who would have commissioned a room like that? It was something that she very much wanted to know. And not just for professional reasons.

Finally, she nodded. She'd made her decision. 'Of course I'll come with you,' she told the driver. 'I just need to put some clothes on.'

She raced back into the bedroom and dragged the crumpled jersey dress back over her head, much to Steve's astonishment.

'Who's at the door?' he asked insistently. 'I know it's not the bailiffs, Cherry. They wouldn't have waited to be invited in.'

'OK, Sherlock,' she admitted. 'It isn't the bailiffs. It's a secret contact of mine. Seems to think he's got a big story. But if he finds out that you're not the plumber he might get a bit upset. I don't want to risk that. You just stay here and eat the pizza, Steve. And call the police if I don't turn up for work tomorrow morning.'

'What? Tomorrow morning? Where are you going? Are you sure it's safe?' he asked frantically. Cherry planted a kiss on his forehead, assured him that it was at least as safe as getting on the wrong side of Madonna, and followed the chauffeur out to the car, hoping that curiosity didn't really kill the cat.

Of course it was crazy of her to be getting into the car again. I mean, Cherry told herself, last night I needed a lift back from the boondocks. It would have been equally as dangerous to try to set off back to London along an unlit B-road as to get into a complete stranger's car, but that was last night. She had been desperate. She had been drunk. She was neither of those now. What on earth has possessed me, Cherry asked herself as she slipped into the back seat once more. Perhaps Eddie was right. Perhaps she really was an insatiable newshound who couldn't let any mystery lay unsolved.

Perhaps she was just being an idiot.

For all Cherry knew, her instincts as she opened the door to her flat might have been right. What if the chauffeur had come to drive her out into the middle of the countryside to murder her for her all too detailed knowledge of the peculiar house? She looked nervously at the lock on her door. It was still open. She made a rough plan that if the car started to stray out of the limited part of London that she knew, she would fling herself out of it at the first set of unfamiliar traffic lights. She had had a brief crush on a foreign correspondent who had taught her how to do exactly that with the minimum of injury.

In the meantime, she tried to engage the chauffeur in conversation. She asked him how long he had been working for his employer; whether this was the mysterious man's only abode. She hoped that he would let something slip that might give her a clue to the identity of the house's owner. At least then she could scribble her thoughts on to a scrap of paper and tuck it into her knickers so that when the police found her body they would know who to question first.

But the chauffeur would not be drawn. And soon the car drew up outside the white house in Belgravia. Once again, it looked to all intents and purposes as though it hadn't been lived in for weeks, even months. Even the pile of junk mail by the front door was still lying exactly where Cherry had kicked it the night before.

The chauffeur had opened the door for Cherry, but when she looked back to see if he could tell her what she was supposed to do next, where she was supposed to go for a start, the chaffeur had already vanished. Cherry took her house keys from her handbag and held them in her fist for added protection. Then, taking a deep breath, she knocked gently on the interior door and waited for an invitation to enter. When none came, Cherry pushed open the door into the hallway and stepped inside.

No sign of life, but in the previously empty stairway stood a single chair. On the velvet seat of the chair was an envelope, addressed to Cherry in spidery writing. Nervously, she picked it up and opened it, expecting ... well, expecting she knew not what.

At first the hastily scribbled words made no sense at all in the dim light. The stairwell was badly lit by a single candle-laden chandelier that dripped hot wax on to the marble-tiled floor. Cherry held her lighter up close to the paper and read the strangely formal words.

> Miss Cherry Valentine. You are cordially invited to join us for an evening of unusual entertainment.

Cherry snorted with confusion when she read that. Us? Who were they? They had neglected to sign the invitation, of course. And what entertainment? She could see no other guests. Nothing that suggested anything interesting was about to happen. Folding the invitation in half and sliding it into her handbag, she sat down heavily upon the lonely chair. It seemed like the only thing to do. She had been sitting there for a couple of minutes when she heard the unmistakable creak of the cellar door.

Cherry felt her mouth go completely dry. The door was open, just a little, as it had been when she first followed that unlucky stray cat into the darkness. Only this time, she knew for certain that it had not been open when she first entered the house. She had checked that much. And this time, real music – not imagined – floated out towards her from the tiny chink in the doorway.

Breathing heavily, and despite her better judgement, she walked towards the cellar. She held her bag out in front of her as if the flimsy leather satchel might protect her from anything that might want to harm her. Her bare legs trembled with each step.

She knew that she was taking a big risk. No one but the chauffeur even knew that she was in the house. And now she was about to step down into a cellar that could contain God only knew what. Her heart thudded so hard against the walls of her chest that Cherry felt sure that its frenzied beating must be audible to anyone else hiding in the house.

'Hello?' she called out, her naturally confident voice taking on the pathetic air of a mouse's squeak. 'Is anybody there?'

She thought she heard a rustle of skirts as someone, or something, scuttled through the cellar, but no one answered her inquiry.

'Is anybody hiding down here?' she called once more, as she took a first cautious step on to the staircase. She cleared her throat before she carried on in her most strident voice, 'Only I promise you that if someone jumps out on me I will scream the place down and then chop the offending person into a thousand little pieces with my bare hands. I've got a black belt in tae kwon do,' she added. It was a lie of course. But she had been to one lesson of the martial art, and the way she was feeling now, tightly coiled as a spring inside a clock, she felt that she could probably unleash the powers of a superhero on to anyone who upset her. At least, that's what she kept telling herself. Her heart beat even faster.

Soon she was at the bottom of the stairs, blinking in the dim light of the painted room. There was still no one to be seen, but in the flickering light of a hundred candles reflected by the ceiling with its countless tiny mirrors, Cherry could see that someone had rearranged the furniture since her last visit. Across one corner of the room, where the wall was decorated with the painting of a hermaphrodite that had intrigued Cherry so much the previous night, an impromptu stage had been constructed and concealed behind a sumptuous velvet curtain.

So this was where the entertainment was to take place.

'I'm here. What am I supposed to do now?' Cherry asked out loud.

Suddenly, a tiny, tinny voice floated out from a cheap-looking plastic speaker set just to the side of the stage.

'Ladies and gentlemen,' said the crackling voice, which sounded distant and spooky as though it had been recorded at a seance. 'Please take your seats in the auditorium. This evening's show is about to begin.'

'What seats?' Cherry mumbled irritably.

But she didn't have to worry for long. When the temporary curtain suddenly flew back to uncover the stage, Cherry was so shocked by the unexpected movement in the deserted room that she tumbled backwards on to the low bed automatically.

Recovering her breath, she scrambled as far back

as she could, until she found herself pressed against the wall, staring at the stage with a mixture of surprise and abject fear. When she could finally bear to look from behind the cushion that she had instinctively grabbed as an ineffectual shield, she saw that two women stood on the previously empty stage. At least, Cherry assumed at first that they were women. The incredible beauties stood so very still that after a while it didn't seem possible that they were human. Between the women was some sort of box covered with a dark red cloth. Weedy organ music began to build to a crescendo, but still the girls stood motionless, like the carvings on the door that Melissa had taken Cherry behind in her dream.

Then, with a sudden flourish, one of the statuesque women came to life and whipped away the cloth that covered the cage. Cherry, who had been creeping forwards to get a better look at these automatons (for she quickly decided from their lack of eye movement that they must be some sort of puppet), jumped backwards again and covered herself with more cushions. Inside the cage, some kind of creature crouched like a wild animal caught in a hunt. The guardians turned the cage around on a creaking turntable so that their exclusive audience could see the captive's face.

But Cherry didn't want to see it. Terrified by the thought of what might be inside, she made a bolt for the door but found it closed and locked. She rattled on the door handle and hammered on the wood but no one answered. Meanwhile, on the stage, the two women continued to move slowly and impassively as if Cherry were still watching unperturbed. Their lack of reaction to her flight further convinced Cherry that she must be witnessing some kind of puppet show, the freakish like of which she had never seen before.

Not daring to settle back down on the bed, however, and deeply concerned by the fact that she found herself locked in, Cherry sank on to the bottom step so that as soon as whoever had trapped her in this hell-hole returned to see what had happened to her, she would be ready to push her way out past him. On the stage, one of the automatons was lifting the lid of the cage. The creature inside began to straighten its narrow body and climb out. Cherry cowered behind a stairpost, waiting for the terrible truth of the cage's contents to be revealed. From what she had glimpsed in her flight to the door, she thought that it might contain some kind of big cat. Some big cat that hadn't been fed in a week.

Christ, she thought, her mind racing down the most horrifying avenue. I'm going to be some moggy's dinner. No wonder the black cat had been afraid. It had probably smelled its bigger, more dangerous cousin lurking in the shadows. She covered her eyes with her hands and held herself very, very still. And all the time the organ music piped out a cheerful little ditty. Cherry was petrified.

'Look, look and be amazed,' the tinny voice cried out. 'Ladies and gentlemen, you've never seen anything like it. Feast your eyes on the one and only Leopard Boy.'

'I was right,' Cherry muttered. 'I was right. A leopard. Please God, let the door open. Please God, let me escape. I'm sorry I ever came here. But I don't want to be eaten. I don't want to be eaten. I don't want to be eaten.'

Her mantra was interrupted by a growl right next to her ear. Cherry quickly rolled herself into a tight ball and prepared for the worst. She pressed her face hard to her knees and held her breath for ever. This had to be the end, she thought. But it wasn't a sharp-clawed paw that rolled her flat again.

To her immense relief and surprise, when she looked up, expecting to see some yellow-eyed cat staring down at her while it considered where to start biting, she found herself looking instead into the eyes of a young man. Not as young as sixteen, but still perhaps not yet out of his teens. He had been painted all over to resemble a leopard, his smooth young skin covered in black and yellow spots that only seemed to enhance his beauty. For he was beautiful.

Just a painted man. The leopard boy smiled down at Cherry from his position on all fours above her trembling, terrified form. She felt her body physically melt into the hard floor as she assimilated the fact that she wasn't about to be mauled to death. She was lying on the floor at the mercy of a complete stranger in body paint, but she wasn't about to be his dinner. She hoped.

Just then, the boy let out another ear-splitting roar that instantly undid Cherry's nerves again.

'Get off me!' She scrambled out from beneath him and skittered backwards until she was sitting upright against the dusty stairs again. But the boy was already getting up and crossing back to the stage anyway, reacting not to Cherry's anguished screams but to a far more authoratative sound.

One of the glassy-eyed guardians standing on the stage had cracked a long, black leather whip so hard that Cherry was sure she could see sparks fly where the leather had hit the still basement air. The boy clambered up to join her, moving not quite on all fours but in a crouched, feral way that suggested the ability to spring out in attack at the slightest provocation. Cherry, still cowering behind her stairpost, was inordinately relieved when one of the creature's guardians clipped a glittering leash on to the ruby-studded collar around his sinewy neck. The other girl was carrying some kind of muzzle, equally bejewelled, but which looked tremendously cruel. When the young boy growled again, the second guardian slipped the restraint over his head.

Cherry was astounded. She stared unblinkingly at the spectacle unfolding before her. What were they going to do? The boy seemed to strain against his bondage, his eyes wide with anger or fear.

Throwing her bangled arms up into the air as if to elicit applause, one of the guardians suddenly turned a slow, graceful cartwheel along the front of the rickety stage. When she came to a resting position, she took the leopard boy's leash from her partner so that the other girl could make the same languorous move in the opposite direction, while the boy snapped at her flashing heels in passing.

Cherry unwound herself just a little from the safety of the stairs to get a better view. The two women, tall and slender as young trees, were dressed in old-fashioned circus outfits. They had plumes on their elaborate headdresses that brushed the low ceiling of the room they were performing in. Their narrow shoulders were covered by small red and gold capes that stuck out comically behind them as if they might take off at any moment. Their long fishnet-covered legs tapered into strangely tiny feet that were encased in red shoes with vicious looking heels.

As Cherry watched now, the two women turned to the back of the stage and discarded the little capes to reveal slender bodies dressed in low-backed leotards. When they turned to the front once more, they revealed beautiful bare breasts decorated with sparkling motifs in crystal and glitter.

The music seeping from the broken speakers wound lazily towards another climax as the three peculiarly matched figures on the stage began a new set routine. While the tethered leopard boy cowered in the centre of the stage, the women took it in turns to vault and somersault over him. They hardly made a sound, leaping and springing with the agility of monkeys. As they moved, the light of the candles caught the glitter on their bodies and gave the impression that shooting stars were streaking past.

The girls moved quickly. Over and under each other. Sometimes Cherry couldn't see where one girl ended and the other began. Sometimes they arranged themselves with the leopard boy in elaborate poses and balanced there like a human house of cards. Their muscles didn't even seem to flex with the slightest hint of effort.

Once they formed a strange triangle. The leopard

boy, his muzzle now removed again, lay still upon the floor while one girl stood at his head to catch the feet of the other girl who stood on her hands to form the triangle's third side. Then, infinitely slowly, the triangle began to collapse in upon itself. The girl on her feet gently parted the handstand girl's legs and leaned forward to bury her face in her pubis. Simultaneously, the handstand girl arched her back so far that it might break, in order to get the leopard boy's penis inside her glossy red mouth.

Despite herself, despite the fact that she was too scared to move even an inch from her hiding place, Cherry couldn't help but be drawn in by the things she could hardly believe she was seeing. She felt that familiar tugging sensation deep inside. A call to action from her clitoris. This bizarre performance was turning her on. As she peeped out from between her fingers, she saw the carefully orchestrated moves melt into the frenzied tumble of an impromptu orgy. A random tangle of limbs replaced the formal poses as the curious lovers fell upon one another in a blur of lips and legs. At one point, the leopard boy looked straight at Cherry as he let his long pink tongue loll out of his mouth in her direction.

She instinctively put one hand to her throat in a protective gesture. She wasn't sure what subconscious urge had her putting her other hand to her pubis.

Without thinking, Cherry slipped her hand beneath the hem of her dress. As the scene playing out on the stage grew more incredible; as the leopard boy applied his strong tongue to each of the circus girls' bodies in turn, Cherry slipped a single finger inside her vagina. Soon she was sliding it in and out, following the rhythm of the organ music. She ran her other hand through her hair in a frenzied gesture, leaning her head back against the stairpost and allowing her body to drop its guard.

As Cherry brought herself to a climax, the room began to spin around her. The glittering ceiling, the paintings on the walls, the creatures coupling frantically on the stage all melted into a kaleidoscopic rush of colour and noise and light. Cherry felt herself slipping into unconsciousness as she came.

Then the music stopped.

As if some magic switch had been flicked, the two women suddenly straightened themselves up and assumed the positions they had been holding on either side of the cage when the curtains first came up. Their fixed expressions betrayed nothing of the frenzied passion that had thrown them on top of one another moments before. Though the feathers on one girl's headdress hung limp and tattered and the other girl had lost her headdress altogether, taking one's cue from their impassive faces it was as though they had never moved.

With a final growl for Cherry's benefit, the leopard boy curled himself into his cage again and was soon hidden from view by the cloth that had covered him before he was first revealed to his reluctant audience. The candles that lit the cellar seemed to gutter and dim momentarily. When they became bright enough to see by again, the cage was uncovered once more, but where previously there had been a young man, Cherry now found to her astonishment that she was locking eyes with a real leopard.

She screamed.

'Let me out of here,' she yelled, flinging herself hard against the door. She pounded until her fists bled. Her cries weren't answered, of course, but when she turned to check that the stony-faced women hadn't unleashed the beast on her, the leopard had gone. Cherry was alone in the room. The other performers and even the cage had disappeared.

It was a while before Cherry felt confident enough that she was alone to get unsteadily to her feet and walk up to the stage to see if she could find a clue to the truth of what she had just seen. On the gold-painted temporary floor, a single black hair attracted her attention. She held the lone hair up to the light of a candle and knew that it was a whisker. Like a cat's whisker, but far too large for a domestic cat. A leopard's whisker. Cherry closed her fist around the only evidence she had that what she thought she had seen had been real.

'Who are you? What's going on down here?' she cried out.

No reply. Only the halting recorded voice on the crackling tape reminding people to be quiet out of courtesy for people living in the area when leaving the auditorium.

'Leave? That's a joke.' Cherry railed at her unseen jailer. 'You're keeping me a prisoner down here.'

The door at the top of the stairs creaked open as if on cue.

Cherry scrambled to the light of the hallway, desperate not only to get out of the cellar, but also to discover who had locked her in. There was no one to be seen, of course. And she wasn't in the mood to search the other rooms. She snatched up her coat from the single chair and wrapped herself in it as she fled the house.

She was halfway down the street when she became aware of the sound of car wheels crunching along the road beside her. The driver, peaked cap still firmly pulled down over his eyes, wound down the passenger window of his limousine and called out.

'Miss Valentine.'

Cherry kept walking.

'Miss Valentine, I've come to take you home again.'

'I'll take a cab, thanks all the same.'

'Your host wouldn't hear of it,' the driver said smoothly.

'You can tell him that I've had enough of his brand of hospitality,' Cherry informed the driver curtly. 'If I'd wanted to see a freak show, I would have got tickets to see Andreas Eros at the Royal Albert Hall.'

The driver's mouth seemed to twitch upwards at the corners in amusement. 'I'm sure that can be arranged.'

'Don't arrange anything on my account,' Cherry snapped. She started to walk faster but the driver kept his car close behind her.

'So, you didn't enjoy yourself in the slightest this evening?' he asked.

'Very funny. Now are you going to leave me alone or shall I have you arrested for kerb crawling?'

The driver wound the passenger window of his

car back up and drove silently into the distance, leaving Cherry all alone.

She pulled her coat tightly around her and put her head down against the wind for the walk to the nearest taxi rank.

# Chapter Six

*BY THE TIME* Cherry got back to the house, Steve had gone, though he had left behind a scrap of paper with his mobile phone number scribbled on it. The accompanying note said that Cherry was to call him if she got back before midnight. But, of course, it was way past midnight by the time she found the hopeful instruction. She hoped he wouldn't be too upset that he hadn't heard from her.

She ran a bath, sitting on the edge of the tub contemplatively as the water rose and ylang ylang scented bubbles billowed up to meet her. She sank down gratefully, feeling the warmth of the water seep into her bones. She felt tired, ready to keel over in fact, but her mind was still racing. She couldn't help but go over and over the things she had seen that night.

Was it simply that the painted boy had been such a good actor that she thought she had seen a real leopard? What kind of lunatic would lock a woman in a room with a real big cat after all? No, Cherry decided, the leopard hadn't been real. She had been the victim of some elaborate trick. But why would someone have gone to so much trouble to play such a trick on her?

If the idea was to keep her from talking about the discoveries she had made the previous night then her mysterious host's plan wasn't working. Burning with a mixture of anger, humiliation and plain old curiosity, Cherry was now utterly determined that she would discover who had put her through such emotional agonies and make them wish they hadn't bothered. A weird sex den in such a smart part of town would keep her paper going for weeks.

Cherry resolved that she would start researching the place at the office first thing in the morning. Someone with so much money that he was able to keep such a huge house in Belgravia at his disposal – not to mention a coterie of servants who wouldn't have seemed out of place on the books of any model agency and seemed happy to do anything to please their master's guests – couldn't possibly have escaped the notice of the press entirely.

The following morning, Cherry was on time for work for the first time in months. She was relieved to discover that Eddie had sent Steve into the city on an errand so he wasn't there to question her when she arrived at the office. Explaining to Eddie that she was on to a hot story but couldn't explain exactly how hot, Cherry set to work finding out just who had made such a fool of her the previous night.

First, she contacted the land registry to find out

whose name the house was registered under, but the only answer she got was a Mr Smith. Not even Smyth or Smythe with an 'e' which might have narrowed the field just a little. Not much help there.

By the end of the day, she thought she had checked every possible avenue and yet she had come up with no answers at all. She couldn't find an entry for the mysterious Mr Smith of Belgravia in the telephone directory. There were no snippets about mysterious comings and goings in Eaton Place in the clippings library. And the local council hadn't received any complaints related to the nocturnal activities of large carnivorous animals. Nothing. In fact they sounded rather amused at the idea. Perhaps she had imagined it after all.

Cherry was just about to scream with frustration when Steve walked into the library with her post.

'I thought you ought to take a look at this lot before you went home,' he said, sliding into the desk beside her and laying his hand on her knee beneath the cover of the desk top. 'You never know, you might have a great story to follow up.'

'Steve, have you ever had any post yourself?' Cherry said, picking up an envelope that was addressed to her in bright green handwriting. 'If someone's got a story so hot that its burning a hole in their conscience, I guarantee you that they will ring the newspaper right away, not scribble me a long letter on recycled lined A4 paper in green biro. And then send it by second class post.' She handed him the letter which started with the words, 'Repent your sins and accept the Lord'. Steve grew more shocked as he read the threats of eternal damnation which followed, but Cherry was used to people taking exception to her unique view on the world as portrayed in her column.

'One of the work experience boy's most important jobs is to make sure that none of Mr Green Biro's letters ever get to me,' she continued. 'Not even if he says he knows the whereabouts of the second coming, which this guy does, frequently. Writing in green biro is a sure sign of madness and it's your job to protect me from the loonies.'

'And what are my other jobs?' he asked, meeting her eyes challengingly as he squeezed her knee beneath the table. Cherry felt a familiar tickle of anticipation deep inside her stomach. 'I missed you last night,' he told her. 'What time did you get back?'

'Late,' said Cherry.

'Where were you? What were you doing?'

'I told you before I left. A spot of investigative journalism.'

Steve's hand crept further up her leg.

'I was worried,' he told her.

'That's nice.'

'I don't suppose you're going to tell me about it?'

'You suppose right, Sherlock.'

'But perhaps we can pick up where we left off last night when you were so suddenly called away?' He raised his eyebrows suggestively.

Cherry felt her internal organs melt into one big hormonal mush. All those times she had accused men of being led by their penises . . . But she wanted to feel someone's arms around her so badly just then. She wanted to be held and protected. The previous night's strange events had left her feeling ever so slightly raw about the heart. Ever so slightly in need of physical comfort.

'Where can we go?' Steve whispered hotly in her ear.

Cherry glanced at her watch. It was five o'clock already. Though for most of the writers on the paper, things were just getting started in earnest as they prepared for the last minute rush before putting the paper to bed for the night, Cherry knew at least one office which would be empty. The book room.

The book review page of the *Star Times* section had been getting smaller and smaller since the paper was taken over by the new proprietor, who announced that the *Daily Mercury* was going to be the people's paper and that the only thing his kind of people read were the headlines and the sports page. Much as the staff on the books page protested that he was wrong, that they got at least three letters a week thanking them for their thoughtful recommendations, the proprietor would not budge from his proletarian pronouncement, and now the books section was down to reviews of three mass market paperbacks every Friday. Rumours were rife that the staff working on the page would soon be cut from two full-time to half a part-timer. Cherry had signed the petition against such a terrible cut.

Not that she was particularly bothered if one of the books staff never darkened the doors of the *Daily Mercury* office again. Nick Henry had set his sights on Cherry the moment the fresh-faced intern, straight from journalism school, had put her pens in the desk-tidy opposite his. She had started off on the books desk, and at first was enormously flattered by the care Nick Henry took to ensure that the little pieces she was allowed to write appeared in the paper without spelling mistakes or grammatical errors.

In fact, she soon began to look forward to that moment in the day when, as he ran his red pen through the extraneous words in her copy, Nick would lean over her shoulder and press his hard chest against her back. It wasn't long before he was pressing something else, even harder, between her quivering legs.

Though she wasn't exactly a virgin when she arrived at the *Daily Mercury* – could you spend three long college years on a corridor full of rugby players without touching one or two of them and being touched rather more roughly in return – Nick was the first man to break through to Cherry's heart. She knew that she loved him even before they slept together. After their first night together on his futon in Highgate, it was as if she could no longer see any other men when she opened her eyes in the morning. It was as if she could see no one else at all, in fact. She drifted round the newspaper offices on fact-finding missions for Nick like a naïve medieval prince carrying out the challenges that would entitle him to the fair princess's hand.

The nine to five was no longer drudge for her. Not when Nick rewarded her for every good piece she wrote with a quick shag in the books cupboard. Even as he put red lines through her dangling participles or ticked her off about a split infinitive, he would be sliding his hand up her leg, or seeking out a way to slip his hand into her knickers without attracting the attention of Graham, the other reviewer. Nick would nod his consent to the review's appearance in the paper and tell Cherry to go to the book cupboard to choose her next project. The unwritten rule was that he would join her moments later with his hard-on already pulling the creases out of the front of his baggy grey trousers.

Once, after a particularly close shave when Graham strolled across the office to borrow the Tipp-ex while Nick had two inky fingers up Cherry's wet vagina, Nick had taken her so roughly that an entire shelf of hardbacks had tumbled down on top of them as they shagged. The falling books hadn't hurt so much, but the corner of the collapsing shelf caught Cherry on the back of the head as it fell. Bleeding profusely and on the edge of passing out with concussion, she had been rushed to the accident unit of the nearest hospital. Nick had refused to go with her, saying that it would look too suspicious. Instead, he told the kindly receptionist who doubled as a first aid officer that he had found Cherry passed out on the floor in the books cupboard when he went to fetch a Booker prize winner to review. He had no idea what had happened to her, of course.

Cherry understood that Nick wanted to protect both their reputations in an office whose daily business was a traffic in scandalous gossip. But when she heard the true version of her accident from behind a cubicle door in the ladies' loo a couple of days later, she realised that her chivalrous knight in shining armour was nothing but a rusty tin man. Heartless. No one should have known the truth about their illicit relationship but Cherry and Nick. Cherry hadn't said anything to anyone so it stood to reason that Nick must have done. It certainly seemed that the story as she heard it now was heavily weighted in his favour.

'She's been coming on to him ever since she arrived,' said Lois, the editor's secretary.

'Bloody disgrace. When does his wife get back from covering that story in Mogadishu?' asked Marla, who commissioned features on fashion and beauty.

Cherry felt as though she had been punched in the gut. What wife? Nick had told her that the women's clothes she saw lying about his flat were his own. She had found it incredibly exciting to think that she was sleeping with a real live transvestite.

The relationship ended less than five minutes after that fatal conversation was overheard. Waiting for the gossipers to leave the loos so that she could crawl out of her cubicle unnoticed, Cherry almost felt her heart harden. She vowed that no one would treat her so badly again. No one would take her love for granted. No one would leave her feeling such a fool. The Cherry Valentine who walked out of the ladies' room that day was a thousand times removed from the naïve intern who had equated Nick's need for sex with adoration. From that day forward she would be the only heartbreaker she knew.

She had pretty much kept her resolve since that life-changing moment. She hadn't had her heart broken since. That said, she hadn't allowed herself to accept the possibility that anyone might truly love her again either.

But once she had taken off her rose-tinted spectacles to better concentrate on the business of becoming a proper journalist instead of someone's love slave, she suddenly found that the path upwards had always been there, in front of her nose. Within three years she had her own column in the newly revamped *Star Times* supplement, which now took up twice the space that the pretentious book reviews were allocated. Nick regularly sent a photocopy of her own column to her through the internal post – with all her grammatical errors and spelling mistakes underlined and identified in spiteful red biro. Now she merely tossed any envelope addressed in his scrawly handwriting straight into the bin.

She smiled wickedly as she picked up the red biro on Nick's unoccupied desk and dropped it on to the floor so that she could sit with her bare ass on his pale pink blotter. The pen landed on her discarded knickers – a little triangle of orange silk bordered by black lace that matched the bra Steve could just see at the deep v-neck of her tight black sweater. The bra that had turned Steve on at their very first meeting.

Thank God fashion dictated that all the girls in the office were wearing almost floor-length skirts that month, thought Cherry, as she hitched her own skirt up just high enough for Steve to see the dark promise of her vagina through the shadow.

She was sitting with her back to the office door. Steve faced the door and promised to give her plenty of warning if anyone approached while they were getting busy.

Cherry pulled Steve towards her, so that he stood between her thighs, and began to toy with the worn metal button at the top of the fly on his jeans. Though she hadn't yet touched him beyond a reciprocal knee squeeze in the library and this first clumsy fumble with his buckle, Steve already had a raging hard-on, which tented the soft denim about his crotch. Cherry ran her hand along the ridge of his erection as she kissed his soft girlish lips. As their lips touched, Cherry felt his penis twitch beneath her palm. It seemed almost as eager to be set free as she was to feel its warm naked weight in her hands again.

She struggled to open the metal buttons of his jeans as they kissed, realising quickly that Steve wasn't wearing any underwear either. Before all the buttons were undone, his hard-on escaped its denim prison and throbbed proudly in full view. Cherry curled her warm hand around its shaft and began to manipulate him quickly as he simultaneously slipped his hand up the back of her sweater to unhook her bra.

The thought that they might be interrupted at any moment was an added aphrodisiac. It made everything so frantic. So urgent. They knew they couldn't undress entirely, and having sex with half her clothes still on was one of Cherry's favourite fantasies. It was so naughty. It reminded her of having a quick one with her sixth-form boyfriend on a single bed in her poster-covered bedroom while her parents watched *Coronation Street* in the sitting room below. Illicit and ever so slightly dangerous. If they got caught it could be the end.

Steve grunted as he slipped his shaft easily inside the warm wet welcome of her pussy. Cherry had been getting wet since they made the decision to leave the library for somewhere quiet, and now she groaned in ecstasy at the feeling of his hard penis stretching the walls of her vagina all the way to her cervix. Quickly, they were moving like a couple of animals. Steve crashed his pelvis against hers while never taking his mouth off her tender lips.

Cherry grasped the back of Steve's head as her orgasm grew inside her like a shimmering bubble of ecstasy. She could feel it increasing the pressure inside her skull, driving her faster towards a climax. Throughout the rest of her body other smaller bubbles were rising like the fizz in a bottle of champagne. Each thrust from Steve's penis pushed her closer to the point at which the cork would finally fly out and her orgasm overflow.

When the moment arrived, Cherry threw her head back to shout. Steve quickly jammed his fingers into her mouth. She bit down hard in her effort to keep quiet, her eyes wide as if they too were trying to shout. Steve stuffed his free hand into his own mouth as he came. His eyes betrayed a mixture of pain and soaring excitement as Cherry bit down even harder while his penis pumped frantically into her cunt.

It had been fast, furious and fantastic. There was not even time for their hearts to slow to a reasonable pace before Cherry retrieved her knickers from the waste paper basket and Steve was zipping himself back up.

'We could do it again,' he said, pressing her hand to the front of his trousers.

Cherry smiled. 'I don't think so. It's too risky.'

'I like risky.'

'So do I,' she assured him. 'So do I. But not right now.'

'Is this the most wicked thing you've ever done?' Steve asked then.

Cherry wiped a smudge of lipstick from his chin and smiled. 'No. It's one of the most pleasurable things I've ever done. But the most wicked thing I've ever done is hypnotise my driving instructor so that he'd make me pass my test.'

Steve laughed. 'That's not true is it? You can't hypnotise people can you? How did you do it?'

'Do you think I'd tell you?' Cherry grinned. 'I'd lose all my power.'

Steve seemed happy with that. 'Can I stay with you tonight?' he asked suddenly.

Cherry found herself nodding in assent before she realised what he was actually asking to do.

'Great,' he said. 'Do you fancy getting something to eat before or after we go to the Andreas Eros show?'

Cherry paused in the act of smoothing out a stockinged leg.

'What show?'

'The Andreas Eros show,' he repeated. 'A unique blend of magic and suspense to make even the most hardened cynic believe that miracles might just happen. At least, that was what the publicity blurb said. You had two tickets arrive this morning. Does that mean that I can come too?'

'What?'

Cherry hadn't spotted the tickets. What on earth was that arsehole magician up to now? Sending her tickets to see his show after he had sworn that if she came within six feet of him or any of his entourage again with her poison pen he would have an injunction slapped on her before she could say 'scoop'.

'I wasn't going to go to that show, actually,' she told Steve flatly.

'Really? I would have thought it was compulsory viewing for you. I overheard Eddie on the phone to the man himself this morning. Eddie promised that the paper would send someone along to give Eros a more accurate review of his show than he got last time.'

'Then you can go and write one,' she said, tugging on her knickers only to find that she had put them on inside out. She pulled them off again, barely able to contain her irritation at the implication of Eddie's smarmy conversation with the magician.

'I think he meant you,' said Steve in his best attempt to be tactful. 'The tickets were biked to you specially, Cherry. I think you ought to reconsider. They were marked with your name.'

'I know he meant me,' she said snappily. 'But I've got a much more important story to cover at the moment. You can do me a favour again, can't you Steve?' she wheedled, seizing upon the opportunity to avoid seeing either the show or Steve. 'The Albert Hall holds thousands. He'll never know that I wasn't there in person. You can watch the show for me and tomorrow morning we'll write up your review together. How about that? I will make it up to you,' she said, planting a dry kiss upon his cheek. 'I promise.'

'I want to spend more time with you,' said Steve plaintively.

Cherry nodded as though she had heard and agreed.

'I think we've got something really special,' he continued.

Cherry looked out at the street from behind the dusty slatted blinds of the book room to avoid Steve's eyes.

'Don't you agree?'

'Yeah, yeah. You know I do,' she told him as she snatched up her bag and pushed past him into the corridor. 'Hang about here for a while, could you? It wouldn't do either of our reputations any good to be seen coming out of this room together.'

She bit her tongue after she said it, well aware that she was almost exactly echoing the instructions that had once been given to her by a certain Mr Nick Henry. But she didn't look back at Steve's dejected figure as she strutted down the corridor. She knew he would be standing exactly as she had once stood herself in that doorway. Head down. Shoulders slumped. Funny how making love can leave you feeling so much colder than if you had never done it at all, Cherry mused as the lift door swooshed open and she stepped inside.

# Chapter Seven

*CHERRY MANAGED TO* get out of the office for the night without seeing either Steve or Eddie on the way. She felt guilty about leaving Steve alone in the book room in such an abrupt manner after he had made love to her so exquisitely. But the way he had banged on about her *having* to see the Eros show almost justified the manner in which she had left him standing there without so much as a tender kiss goodbye.

Two days into her fling with Steve, Cherry knew that she had probably made a big mistake by giving in to his sweet temptation. It was clear he felt that a lot more had already passed between them than bodily fluids. His proprietorial manner, the bossy way in which he was already trying to organise her life for her, suggested that he was investing a lot more emotion in their relationship than she, and the responsibility of someone else's feelings was something Cherry definitely didn't need just then.

Pouring herself a glass of red wine while she ran another bath, she sat down on the peeling windowsill of her summer-yellow kitchen and looked out on to the chilly London street outside. A hard frost which hadn't properly thawed all day lent the grubby tarmac surface of the pavement a glamorous glittery sheen. The bare-branched trees in the garden looked as though they had been given a frosting of sugar like the edge of a fancy cocktail glass.

As she watched a wind-blown couple making their way home through the winter wonderland, arms wrapped around each other for warmth, laughing at private jokes as they struggled to stay upright on the ice, Cherry suddenly felt profoundly lonely. She knew that all she had to do was dial his number and Steve would be round to comfort her in minutes, but somehow she also knew that the physical presence of a reasonably attractive body would no longer be enough.

Cherry had been trying to work out what felt wrong ever since she had walked away from Steve's crest-fallen face. Steve certainly knew how to turn her on with the expert stroking of his hands and the professional touch of his lips. He could make her come in crazy positions that she didn't think her body was capable of without breaking bones. She could have looked at him for hours. His perfect body. His wonderful face. She would never get tired of them. But when they weren't entangled in bedsheets or coupling frantically against a rickety desk, Cherry was surprised to realise that she found Steve himself somewhat boring.

When he tried to have a go at her about missing the Andreas Eros show, she hadn't been worried at the thought of upsetting him by refusing to go along. She didn't ache to prove him wrong when he pointed out a flaw in her character. She didn't want to impress him so much with her all-round wonderfulness that he never looked at another woman again.

She could take it or leave it. That was the problem.

It wasn't that Cherry wanted to feel that ambivalent about anyone. She had considered the possibility that she had been throwing herself gleefully into the zipless fucks she had been having recently because she didn't want any more involvement beyond the physical. She knew enough about psychology to believe that you only get what you really want out of life. If you're not ready for commitment then it doesn't come in your direction. You just don't send out the right signals.

But she also knew that she didn't want to have incredible sex with a guy and then still be able to walk away without any regret that it might not happen again. She wanted someone to affect her so deeply, so completely, that being without that person was a real trial, not a minor inconvenience to the pursuance of her energetic sex-life.

She tried to remember when she had last felt that way about anyone. Nick Henry? The book cupboard bonker? Was he the last person to make her feel that great? He had certainly hurt her enough to suggest that she had been in love with him when they split up. But had she really been so head over heels? Making love in Nick's office that afternoon hadn't given her the frisson of delicious revenge that she thought it might. Perhaps she was over him at last. Yet surely you could never be over someone you had truly loved?

Was there anyone before Nick Henry? She had

met men at college who made her cry as often as they made love to her, but she had long since worked out that half of the emotion she had interpreted at the time as heart-ache had in fact been rage against the stinging humiliation of being dumped. She couldn't even remember the names of those guys now. They were faceless. Incredible to believe that anyone who had made her come then made her cry could fade from her memory so completely.

Cherry took a last sip from her glass of red wine and sniffed back a little tear of self-pity that had been threatening to break free and roll down her nose. Was she destined to live the rest of her life as the hard-hearted person she had resolved to become after Nick's betrayal? Would she never meet anyone who could break through?

Day after day she met people whom she thought she could have slept with. Handsome men. Funny men. Men who would shower her with the kind of gifts and compliments that other girls would have overlooked a thousand little flaws for. But no one Cherry felt she could have loved . . . Or had she? Would she even know if the ideal man walked up and pinched her on the arse? Her mother had often assured her that relationships were something to be worked at. Love could grow from a friendship, she claimed. You might not know if you didn't give the underdog a chance, and Steve was the underdog in Cherry's life just then. She wasn't convinced. She was still waiting for a lightbulb flash of recognition that she'd met her soulmate, the big bang. She hadn't had one of those with Steve. At least not the sort of big bang she was thinking of at that moment.

Where was her dream prince, she snorted. It was easy to find someone who looked as though they fitted the job description. Finding someone that didn't turn back into a frog after she kissed him was going to be the hard part.

'But Steve definitely isn't the one,' she confided to Goldie as she sprinkled a few flakes of fish food into his bowl. 'At least, I don't think so. If only I could be like you, eh, fish-face? If only I had a thirty second memory, I'd always be happy because I wouldn't be able to remember if there was anything more fulfilling than the last shag I had.'

Cherry was in the bath when the phone rang. She wrapped herself in a fluffy towel and hurried to answer it, fully expecting her caller to be Steve. After her maudlin five minutes on the windowsill, a flick through the latest issue of *Cosmopolitan* while she lay soaking in the bath had made Cherry reconsider her bleak outlook on love. Perhaps Steve could be moulded into the perfect lover given time and extensive detailed instructions. As she walked through the sitting room, she gave herself a sneaky appraisal in the scratched old mirror over the fireplace. Not bad for a girl just the wrong side of thirty. All her own teeth and a toy boy, she smiled.

'I'm wet and ready for you,' she growled into the phone.

'Er, right,' said the caller.

'Steve?' Cherry asked, her voice already rising to a wobble.

'No. It's Eddie.'

Cherry crashed the phone receiver against her forehead in embarrassment.

'I thought you were someone else,' she explained hurriedly.

'That much is pretty clear,' said Eddie. 'What are you doing at home, Miss Valentine?'

'I was in the bath,' she said.

'Weren't you meant to be somewhere tonight?'

She gritted her teeth. Eddie obviously meant to ask her why she wasn't at the bloody Andreas Eros show.

'I wasn't feeling too good when I left the office,' she lied. 'I thought I might come home, take a few painkillers and see if I felt up to the second half. No point trying to write a fair review with a headache. And I know how much he deserves a fair review.'

Eddie grunted in agreement. 'Well, how are you feeling now?'

'Much better.'

'That's good, because I need you to go somewhere else for me as soon as you're ready.'

'What?' Cherry groaned. 'Did I say I felt better, Eddie? All of a sudden I'm feeling a bit faint again. It's cold outside.'

'I've had a tip off,' he told her, ignoring any excuses. 'There's a special party being thrown tonight. Going to be crawling with celebs. I need you to be there.'

'Really? Who's throwing the party?'

'That's what you need to find out. The invitations have been sent out anonymously.'

'Probably just a PR stunt by some boring drinks firm trying to pique our interest,' Cherry said flatly.

'Maybe. But maybe not. There are some big people about who might just throw a party anonymously to make us think just that in a cunning double-bluff. But they're not putting us off the trail this time. I've got a feeling that this is going to be the party of the year.'

'You always say that,' Cherry laughed.

'This time I mean it.'

'Why can't you go instead?'

'Because it needs someone with your special charm. Besides, the invitation I have managed to procure belongs to a woman and I don't look good in a dress. Don't let me down, Cherry. Tonight your name is Janina Easton.'

'Nice name. Whoever she is. Where have I got to go?'

'A driver will come to collect you.'

'Can't you just give me the address?' She didn't want to find herself tied down to leaving the house before she wanted to.

'Nope. There's no address on the invitation. You have to ring this number and ask for a car to be sent round. I've already called it for you to save you the bother. Fifteen minutes be OK? It's a masked ball. Very grand-sounding. Everyone will be arriving by limousine apparently. Dress up. Your mask will come with the car.'

Eddie put the phone down before Cherry could protest.

She replaced the receiver at her end and cursed her boss. The last thing she wanted to do that night was gatecrash a party. Even if it was going to be the 'party of the year'. Only a month before, Eddie had claimed that his fortieth birthday party would be the 'party of the year'. The event had consisted of three bowls of Twiglets and a six-pack in the office. If that was Eddie's idea of the greatest bash on earth, then there was a strong chance that the only celebs at the party he was sending Cherry to that night would be redundant weather-girls in search of a game show. She often found that she was more well-known than the celebs she was supposed to be stalking.

But Eddie Bennett was her boss. And now that he knew she hadn't gone to the Andreas Eros show, Cherry found herself utterly at his whimsical mercy. Reluctantly, she gave up on the idea of returning to her lovely warm bath and began the process of dressing herself up for that night's mission.

She stood in front of her wardrobe and ran her fingers over the battalion of black dresses within. She had a monochrome wardrobe designed to take her to any occasion. Her uniform, she called it. But would any of the dresses be good enough for a masked ball? She discarded three stretchy Lycra dresses that she wore for clubbing and book launch parties. And the dress she saved for celebrity funerals was just a bit too dowdy for anything but burying celebs. That left a strapless number that she had inherited from a fashion editor who had moved from the *Daily Mercury* to a far glossier paper.

Cherry held the strapless dress with its voluminous skirts against her body and luxuriated in the soft caress of the silk against her naked skin. It was a beautiful dress, but when she first eagerly accepted it as the fashion editor cleared out her cupboard, she hadn't really imagined that she would ever find an occasion quite special enough to merit taking the dress out of its wrapping paper. The heart-shaped bodice that had been too tight for the previous owner seemed to have been made to measure for Cherry, pushing up her firm, round bosoms until she had a cleavage to die for. The bodice sparkled with hundreds of tiny Swarkovski crystals that threw speckles of light up on to Cherry's face, like the mirrors on the ceiling of the secret cellar room, as she twirled across her bedroom floor.

Perhaps tonight was the occasion, she thought, as she came to a halt in front of the wardrobe doors with the dress still held up to her chest. She chewed her lip thoughtfully. It wouldn't be much good if she found herself having to climb over a razor wire fence at three o'clock in the morning to escape an angry bouncer. On the other hand, if she thought that way every time an opportunity to wear the ballgown came up, she might find that she was too fat to get into it by the time she finally plucked up the courage.

Cherry stepped into the dress reverently. She wasn't sure what kind of underwear one should wear under a ballgown like this and so she wore none, she didn't want to spoil the line. And she didn't have anything decent or clean. Normally, she would have been a little nervous about attending a February party without her knickers, but the dress fitted her so perfectly that she had no concerns about slipping out of its confines at some inopportune moment.

'What do you think, Goldie?' she asked the fish when she finally managed to fasten the last tricky button on the bodice. 'I don't scrub up too badly, do I?' Goldie mouthed his approval.

She piled her hair high on her head and secured it with a pin that sported a huge red fabric amaryllis. Then she slipped her narrow feet into the nicest pair of shoes she could find at the bottom of her wardrobe and started to paint her face. As she covered her cheeks, still flushed pink from the warmth of the bath, with a layer of porcelain-white powder, Cherry began to feel a little more enthusiastic about the night's mission. By the time she painted on a glossy red mouth, she couldn't wait for the car to arrive.

The nervous fluttering of her heart suggested that perhaps this was what she had been missing lately. Mystery. Romance. A masked ball had both of those. Perhaps tonight she would have her lightbulb moment with a masked avenger, she laughed as she pulled a comb through the front of her hair to complete the effect.

She was admiring herself in the mirror when the doorbell rang to announce that her car had arrived. Snatching her velvet purse from the table beside the door – the purse which contained her emergency journalist kit: a dictaphone and a camera, both small enough to be secreted almost anywhere – Cherry flew out into the lobby, eager to get going. She slipped on an icy patch by the front step and skidded to a halt, her nose in the driver's broad chest.

'Excited?' he laughed, taking her by the shoulders and setting her back on her high heels.

Cherry pushed her hair out of her eyes and stared

in amazement at the familiar man before her. Her driver for that night was *the* driver. The driver who had brought her back from the Promised Pleasures party and delivered her to the white house again the following night.

'I've come to take you to the party,' he told her, with a little flicker of amusement at the corner of his mouth when he too recognised her.

'I guessed. Do you work for many people?' she asked.

'Just the one.'

The driver turned and walked towards his car. Cherry was still standing on the front step of her house when he opened the passenger door for her to climb inside. *Just the one.* The relevance of the words took a few moments to sink in.

'Where is this party?' she called.

'I think you know the house, *Miss Easton*,' the driver said with heavy sarcasm.

Cherry opened her mouth to say something in reply but nothing clever emerged. For a moment she stood on the front step, opening and closing her mouth like Goldie, until the driver coughed to attract her attention to the matter in hand.

'Are you coming? I've got a few people to pick up tonight,' he told her.

Despite her misgivings, Cherry nodded and followed him to the car. Eddie had called to say that this was going to be a big party, and now the driver was saying that he had lots of other people to pick up. Even if she did end up at that weird house again, it seemed that she wouldn't be alone that night. It was safe, wasn't it? On the other hand, whether it was safe or not, Eddie Bennett would be expecting some kind of report in the morning.

'I'm glad you changed your mind,' said the driver.

'It's a masked ball, isn't it?' Cherry asked as she climbed into the deep leather seat she was becoming rather used to.

'Your mask is beside you,' the driver explained.

She turned to see a box next to her. She opened it quickly, eager to see what she would be wearing that night. Inside the box, swathes of gossamer fine tissue paper enveloped a half-face porcelain mask for her eyes. Cherry lifted it out with infinite care. It was almost certainly an antique; a painted face like the ones she had seen in Venice on a family holiday many years before. The serene symmetrical features of this particular mask were decorated with a pretty skyscape. Friendly white clouds drifted across a summer blue background.

'This is beautiful,' she murmured, still not daring to hold the delicate piece to her face.

'It was chosen especially for you.'

Cherry felt a frisson of pride at the implication that someone had thought such a beautiful mask suitable for her.

'Your employer has great taste.'

'Thank you,' said the driver, as though he was accepting the compliment for himself.

'Is that his line of work? Art?' she dared to ask.

The driver laughed to show that he had guessed immediately that she was probing him for information. Trying to catch him out.

'I'm afraid I can't tell you, but perhaps he'll reveal all to you himself one day.'

Cherry settled back into the leather seat once again and smiled behind the mask. A white ribbon held it firmly in place against her face.

'Will you be joining the party?' she asked him. 'You wouldn't even need a mask with that hat of yours always pulled down over your eyes.'

'We're here,' he said, getting out of the car to open the door for her.

He didn't answer Cherry's question.

With the mask hiding most of her face, as instructed on the elegant invitation, Cherry climbed the familiar steps to the forbidding front door of the white house.

How different it was tonight though. Even as she lifted her hand to rap on the knocker, the door was opened for her. Two smartly liveried doormen in plain black masks that left their mouths uncovered bowed low as Cherry passed between them into the hall she had last seen in a blur as she ran through it at a gallop, fleeing from heaven only knew what creature in the basement. Now the hallway was thronged with people; gorgeously dressed, chattering people, all hiding behind beautiful masks, though none, she noticed with a small shiver of pride, as beautiful as hers.

She drifted around the room, peering at the strangers, wondering if any of the anonymous masks hid real faces that she knew. An air of excitement and anticipation filled the crowded room. As if to make up for the fact that their facial expressions were hidden, or at least largely obscured, the guests gesticulated and touched each other far more than they would otherwise have done. Cherry wondered what everyone was expecting to happen. Was she the only one who had been to the house before, or were all her companions familiar with its hidden secrets? Would there be any unusual entertainment that night? It was with a slightly surprising feeling of disappointment that she noticed that the door to the basement was being blocked from use by a string quartet.

In fact, it seemed like a normal enough party, the kind one might expect to encounter in any of the tall white houses along that expensive and exclusive street. Cherry overheard conversations about heavy traffic, house prices; one woman enquired about another guest's wife. So much for scandal. She was ready to give up on any kind of gossip and leave when the red-masked waiters who had previously been distributing tall glasses of champagne from their huge silver platters emerged from the kitchen with a new cargo on display.

'Would you care to help yourself?' one asked.

Cherry was glad that she had a mask to cover her surprise when the waiters started to weave in and out of the chattering crowd, not with champagne or canapés, but condoms. Piles of condoms. Coloured, flavoured, ribbed, glow in the dark. The waiters offered the guests a choice of protection as if they were offering a choice of caviar or salmon.

However, no one but Cherry seemed in the least bit surprised by this sudden development in proceedings. Men and women alike helped themselves to the colourful cellophane-wrapped cargo without flinching. Two girls to her left compared the relative merits of two differently flavoured sheaths. And she had to stop herself from laughing out loud when a man to her left, who could barely see his feet beneath the vast expanse of his belly, let alone find his penis, picked up three novelty glow in the dark condoms and then had the cheek to pinch Cherry's bottom.

'Would you care to help me find out how these work?' he asked.

Shaking her head vehemently, she quickly moved away to a safe corner of the room and flattened herself against the wall, as if by staying still enough she might escape detection in the rush for partners. Meanwhile, the anticipation of the guests was suddenly spilling over into frantic action. All around, couples were pairing up and drifting off to private corners. Men and women invited others to join them. Threesomes. Foursomes. Girl on girl. Boy on boy. There didn't seem to be any real rules as to who ended up with whom.

Cherry watched the developing scene with a growing sense of incredulity. Having given up on winning a piece of her affection, the fat man actually bodily picked up a slight lady wearing a red dress and a cat's face mask and threw her over his shoulder to climb the grand stairs. The string quartet soon became a trio, and then a duo as the musicians were picked off one by one. Finally, the last lone violinist followed a girl wearing a duck-face mask and little else into the kitchen. Cherry was practically alone in the hallway, ignored, standing in her corner; the last party-goer left in a game of musical affairs.

Orgy.

Cherry breathed the word like a mantra.

It was arguably the most longed-for and welcome

word in a tabloid journalist's vocabulary. Better than discovering that a squeaky clean footballer has a problem with recreational drugs. Better than 'major government fraud' or 'serial killers'. Better than discovering that someone high up in the government *is* a drug-using serial killer.

An orgy. Everybody wants to hear about one. Everybody wants to go to one. But not many people want to have to admit as much. Especially not in print. And especially not if they hold any position of importance in society. It was truly a reporter's paradise to have stumbled upon one, and in *such* genteel surroundings. There was bound to be someone important getting up to something scandalous here.

Cherry's heart pounded in her chest. For once Eddie had been right. She didn't know where to start with the neat compact camera that she had hidden in her velvet bag. With her mask still over her face, she pulled out the camera and set about trying to find a party guest whose mask had slipped while his or her attention was elsewhere. She heard the sound of a familiar laugh drift out from the first floor room that Cherry knew contained a grand piano. Frantically, she tried to place the laugh. It was a pop star, wasn't it? No, a soap star. That awful braying was the unmistakable laugh of . . .

Before Cherry could open the door to the music room and find out if she had been right, her path was blocked by a strong arm.

She looked up angrily into an impassive golden mask, with features not unlike the ones moulded upon her own. But the stranger would not move from his guard position in the doorway and let her get her exclusive. His mouth, left uncovered by his mask, twisted into a curious smile. A familiar smile.

'Excuse me,' Cherry said irritably, as she backed away from his biceps. 'I'm not interested in . . .'

'In what?'

'In fucking.'

'Then why come to an orgy?' the man asked.

The stranger continued to lean against the door as he ran curious hands down the sides of Cherry's elegant neck and across her smooth bare shoulders. She felt a path of goosepimples spring up in the wake of his fingers. The nape of her neck prickled angrily at his touch.

'I . . .' she began to protest.

'Sssh.'

The stranger touched a finger to her lips. Then he wrapped his arm around her shoulders and began to lead her away from the door. As they walked across the landing, the stranger prised Cherry's camera from her shaking hands and tossed it down the centre of the stairwell.

'Hey!' she protested. She flew to the banister just in time to see her camera shatter into a hundred tiny pieces on the tiled floor below.

'My camera. You . . .'

'You don't need that anymore,' the stranger told her, taking her hand and leading her in the direction of the bedroom Cherry knew only too well.

'Where are you taking me?'

'Just trust me and follow.'

She tried to pull her hand free again, nervous of what she might find behind that bedroom door. As far as she knew, the four poster she had had so much fun in was the only bed in the house apart from the low platform in the cellar. The bedroom would surely be crawling with people making love. Cherry would do a lot for her job, but the one thing she dreaded was being touched by people that she hadn't chosen to touch her. What if the fat man was in there? He'd be all over her. No way on earth was that going to happen. She finally shook her hand free of the stranger's and planted her feet firmly on the landing like an obstinate horse.

'What are you waiting for?' the stranger asked as he pushed the door to the bedroom open.

'I don't think I'm up for this.'

'Up for what?'

Cherry tried to peer around him to see how awful the scene inside actually was. But incredibly, this room – the only room on the landing that actually had a bed – was completely empty. The man stepped inside and beckoned her forward.

'What do you want me to do?' Cherry asked nervously, as she followed him inside. 'I don't . . .'

'I know. You haven't done this kind of thing before, have you?'

'Of course not,' she protested, sounding ludicrously prudish considering the amazing week she had had. Aaron. Steve. She hadn't let any old-fashioned morals get in the way then. But something about this man in the mask was making Cherry's stomach churn. Was it that she was afraid of him? Or attracted? Should she just tell him that she was a journalist in search of a story and make her excuses? That didn't seem like such a great idea, so instead she blustered, 'It's just that . . . I don't know who you are. I mean, I haven't seen your face.'

The stranger nodded. 'And I haven't seen yours. But don't you find it helps you to be less inhibited?'

Cherry snorted at that. She suddenly felt very inhibited indeed. As they talked about how she felt, the man somehow managed to back her right up against the end of the bed. When he reached out to touch her shoulders again, she ducked away from him and collapsed backwards on to the bed in an angry rustle of taffetta.

He sat down next to her and folded his hands in his lap as if to symbolise that he wouldn't make any moves she didn't ask for.

'Isn't this your kind of party then?' he asked.

'I didn't know it was going to be *this* kind of party,' Cherry said.

'Then why did you bring your camera?'

'I like to take photos of parties. All those dressed-up people.'

'Because you're a journalist.' The stranger gave it to her straight.

'How do you know?' she spluttered.

'You were carrying a camera and you weren't taking your clothes off. The only prudes you ever find at an orgy are journalists.'

'You got me bang to rights. I should be off.'

She started for the door. But the man was quicker and again blocked her passage.

'Let me out,' she said.

'I don't want you to go.'

'I'm here to do my job. Now you've broken my camera, I can't.'

'Don't you want to stay to enjoy the party anyway? You're the most intriguing person here tonight.'

He touched the amaryllis in her hair. Cherry jerked her head away from his hand.

'I don't think your host would be very happy to know that there's a journalist in the house,' she ventured.

'I am the host.'

Cherry stared. 'This is your house?'

He nodded.

'Then who the fuck are you?'

'Who wants to know?'

'You know who I am. At least you must know that this isn't the first time I've been here. As your guest.'

The stranger nodded again, still running his hands over her hair.

'I was very impressed by your interior design skills,' she told him, as she slapped his hand away defensively.

'I take it that you're not referring to this room,' her host replied.

'How quick you are.'

'I thought you might enjoy my secret temple.'

'Oh, I enjoyed it,' she snarled. 'It would make a great story.'

'I don't think you really want to write about it though, do you?' he said.

'Why me?' Cherry demanded. 'Why did you have me brought here?'

'I didn't. You chose to come of your own free will. Twice.'

'So the first time your driver brought me back to this house from that party was an accident?'

'You took someone else's lift.'

'I was stuck in the middle of nowhere.'

'Didn't you also break and enter?'

Cherry had to smile at that.

'You scared me last night,' she told him.

'That wasn't my intention.'

'I think I deserve to know who you are.'

The stranger, as inscrutable as his driver, deftly avoided the challenge. 'I had hoped that you would find my little circus show diverting. Though I suppose I shouldn't have been surprised that you didn't enjoy it. I had already heard that you're notoriously difficult to please,' he added.

'I don't know where you could have heard that,' Cherry retorted. 'I think I'm a fair critic of shows that I'm not forced to see through imprisonment. I could have sent the police round.'

He laughed. 'I assure you that the door was open all the time. It has no lock. You just weren't trying hard enough to open it.'

'I could have pulled that door off its hinges.'

The stranger smiled. 'Were you very disappointed with what you saw?'

Cherry found herself hesitating again. 'I wouldn't say that I was disappointed. It was... It was certainly amazing. But I was... I suppose I was just a bit too frightened to stay and applaud,' she admitted.

'Frightened of losing yourself to your desires.'

'Frightened of being shut in a cellar with a wild animal,' she gasped.

'There was no wild animal in the cellar, Cherry. Just a figment of your imagination.'

'I saw it.'

'What we see doesn't always correspond to what is actually there in front of our eyes. Don't you believe in the power of illusion?'

'I don't believe that what I saw last night was an illusion,' she said, remembering the very real whisker she had picked up from the stage.

The stranger inclined his head and looked at her closely from behind his mask. Cherry stared back intently, desperate for what little she could see of his eyes and mouth to remind her of a face she might know.

'Do I know you? I mean, from outside this place?'

'I don't think anyone really *knows* anyone, do you?' he asked.

'Don't try to distract me with riddles, pal. Why did you choose me?' she asked again. 'You obviously know quite a bit about me.'

'Perhaps it was because I thought you might be difficult to impress. I like a challenge.'

Cherry bristled at the implication that she hadn't been as great a challenge as her host had expected.

'Well, now the game is over, isn't it?' she said to him petulantly. 'The challenge is won. You've got me to come here under false pretences, you impressed me with your puppet show, so now you can tell me who you are and let me go home.'

'Don't you think it would be more fun to keep guessing for just a little while longer?'

'No.'

'Oh, Cherry,' the stranger sighed. 'You seem to

have lost all your sense of adventure. Magical things can't happen to people who won't let themselves believe in magic, you know.'

As he said this, he took one of Cherry's elegant hands between his, lifted it to his lips and kissed each of her fingers in turn. Then, he took her ring finger and sucked it into the warm cavern of his mouth, right up to the second knuckle. Cherry couldn't help but close her eyes at the sensation of his tongue against the sensitive flesh of her fingertips. The gesture was almost more erotic than a kiss planted on her lips.

That was to come.

'Can I kiss you?' he asked.

Cherry didn't answer. She opened her mouth to say 'no' but somehow she couldn't bring herself to form the word. Instead, she fixed her eyes on the stranger's. She let him stroke the back of her hand. He tilted his head again in a gesture of appeasement. Her mouth relaxed into a smile.

'I think you're going to kiss me whether I want you to or not,' she told him, and was surprised to find that even as she said those words, she realised that she did actually want him to. Though she didn't know who he was, there was no denying that he was beguiling. With her mask still firmly covering her eyes, she tacitly allowed her lips to brush those of her unknown host. They were warmer than their expression had been until then, softer and smoother than she had imagined.

'That was nice,' she murmured.

'Didn't you always know that it would be?' he replied.

It wasn't long before his tongue probed gently at the roof of her mouth and traced the edge of her teeth. At the same time, his fingers tenderly caressed the back of Cherry's neck and her naked shoulders. The longer this kiss progressed, the more she became aware that he was breaking down her reserve.

Giving in to the moment, she closed her eyes and allowed the kiss to take over her entire body. Her arousal began like a tiny flame flickering into life deep inside her. The flame gave out a fine grey smoke of excitement that curled its way determinedly along every limb. Eventually, she allowed herself to fall slowly back on to the bed, wrapped in the stranger's arms. He lay himself gently on top of her, supporting his weight on his elbows.

The jet beads on the bodice of Cherry's beautiful dress clicked against the small pearl-white buttons on her mysterious host's shirt. It was the kind of shirt that Cherry had always imagined a Victorian poet would wear, its voluminous sleeves billowing luxuriously from narrow cuffs. She could easily feel the contours of his muscles beneath the fine silk from which it had been fashioned.

On his legs, the stranger wore a pair of equally old-fashioned sand-soft suede breeches that tucked neatly inside a pair of shining leather boots. Soon Cherry found herself running her hands greedily over his tightly covered buttocks. She could easily imagine that he was her prince, if she wanted to.

'I watched you in here the other night,' he murmured. 'I watched you lay down on this bed and caress yourself to sleep. What were you thinking about that night? Who were you thinking of?'

Cherry looked up into his eyes and told him honestly, 'I was thinking about a moment like this.'

The stranger sighed with pleasure as she began to undress him. Beneath his white shirt, his broad shoulders were as smooth and hard as marble. Pushing the sleeves off those shoulders, Cherry ran her hands over his biceps. The muscles were flexing beautifully as he held himself steady above her body so as not to crush her with his weight. Her host had a wonderful body, and by the time she started edging his breeches over his narrow hips, she had no doubt that she was enjoying this most unusual encounter. In fact, she was starting to see his point about the mask lowering her inhibitions.

Meanwhile the man covered her breast-bone with kisses, warm kisses that left her skin tingling with delight. She arched her back up away from the mattress so that he could slide his arms beneath her and roll her over on to her front. Then she held her loosened hair out of the way as he pressed yet more kisses to her shoulders. She shivered as he touched his tongue delicately to the nape of her neck then licked a path down to the top edge of her dress. When he had done that, the stranger sat up and stroked his hands down across Cherry's neck, right along her arms to her fingertips. She wondered if this was what it felt like to be a cat. His hands soothed and smoothed her, leaving her longing for his touch.

Soon, she felt his attention move to the buttons that fastened her beautiful dress. As each tiny jet button popped free of its button-hole, she felt a little more exposed. She could almost feel his breath on the skin that had been covered by the black silk, though he was sitting so high above her that it wasn't really possible.

Eventually the dress was completely unbuttoned. Cherry felt her body slacken luxuriously as the restricting bones of the bodice fell away from her waist. The stranger rolled her over on to her back again. When Cherry sat up to kiss him, the bodice fell forward, leaving her perfect breasts naked beneath his hungry eyes.

'Beautiful,' he murmured as he stroked the back of his hand across the peach-soft flesh of Cherry's shivering decolletage. Her nipples stiffened in the wake of his hand. She threw her head back to allow him to see more of her, to touch more of her. To kiss more of her.

His warm mouth moved quickly and hungrily over her breasts. Cherry groaned and sighed in encouragement as he took each of her tiny pink nipples in turn between his teeth. When they began to ache with pleasure, Cherry grasped at the back of his head and pulled his masked face down into her cleavage, where he lapped at the delicious valley between her breasts with his hot tongue. When she was just about ready to spontaneously combust with the intensity of the pleasure of his mouth upon her body, the stranger suddenly stood up.

Lying back on the bed, already feeling deprived by the absence of his hands upon her for even a second, Cherry allowed her eyes to drift down the man's body. His square pectoral muscles flexed invitingly as he tugged the tight boots off, hopping from one foot to the other. When they were at last discarded, the stranger was finally able to remove his trousers properly and the warm shaft that had been straining to be released ever since he had led her into the room, was suddenly revealed to her in its full glory.

He climbed on to the bed again. This time he sat astride Cherry and caressed what little of her face he could see below the mask she wore.

'Do you want me to take the mask off?' she asked him.

He shook his head. Then he moved forward into a kneeling position so that his penis loomed above Cherry's appreciative eyes. She noticed at once that he had tied a golden thread around the base of the long straight shaft. She reached up and ran a curious finger along the thread. The stranger's penis twitched upwards as if to signify its approval of her.

'What is this for?' she asked.

'To prolong the pleasure. I want this to last for ever,' he told her.

Cherry found herself nodding in agreement, before the man moved forward and, tucking his hand beneath her head, lifted her face towards the end of his shaft. Cherry knew instantly what she was to do. She opened her lips and allowed the shaft inside. The salty taste of a tiny drop of crystal clear semen was as delicious as the champagne she had been drinking when the party began.

She ran her tongue quickly across the narrow eye of his penis, eliciting another tiny drop of excitement. She reached up and fondled his balls as she sucked eagerly, enjoying their warmth and weight in her hands. When the stranger sighed with arousal,

Cherry felt suddenly triumphant. She was surprised how much it mattered to her that she turned this man on.

The stranger's penis quickly grew harder, and soon became so engorged with his increasing arousal that the fine golden thread seemed to be cutting into his skin. Cherry struggled to sit up beneath him, her ballgown still around her waist so that she looked like a half-opened chocolate. The man licked his lips as if the thought had crossed his mind too.

'I need to see your face,' Cherry told him again.

'Not yet,' he said. 'When you're ready. I promise.'

'I am ready,' she assured him. 'I want to know who you are.'

'Not yet,' he said, like an echo of himself.

He edged Cherry's dress down over her hips at last. She watched the naked portion of his masked face closely for a flicker of emotion that might betray how he felt about the body his actions had revealed. But she didn't need to look for a flicker; the wide spread of his smile was unequivocal in its praise. Her breathing quickened as he ran his fingers down the length of her body, pausing at the edge of the neat triangle of her pubis to stroke the silky hair.

With his eyes locked on hers, the stranger slipped his hand between Cherry's legs. She gasped, then bit her bottom lip as his fingers brushed against her clitoris. She could feel that she was already wet, ready for this moment. Without needing to be asked, she moved her legs a little further apart so that he could reach her more easily. She held his gaze as he carefully started to push a finger inside her. A blush of arousal crept over her whole body. She felt her cheeks begin to glow. Heat radiated from every pore of her skin, and upon that heat floated the musky scent of her arousal.

As if he wanted to taste that arousal, the man licked at the shallow hollow between Cherry's narrow ribs. She put her hands on his shoulders, then, as carefully and cautiously as she could, moved them to the back of his head. Her fingers had just touched the knot of the ribbon which held his mask in place when he suddenly sat up, defeating her in her quest to unmask him.

'Not yet,' he said once more.

To prevent her from trying to unmask him again, the man took both of Cherry's slender wrists in one of his huge hands and held her arms firmly above her head. This gentle gesture of restraint had the effect not of angering Cherry but of arousing her still further. Her chest heaved upwards as she tried to breathe the man in. The perfume of their entangled bodies swirled in the air around them like incense. As he flicked out his tongue to touch Cherry's again, the taste of his salty saliva in her mouth made her want to curl her legs around his back to underline how much she needed him just then.

With his free hand, the stranger sought out the entrance to Cherry's aching vagina. She closed her eyes tightly as she waited for him to enter her. She felt her body start to open like a flower turning to the sun as his penis nudged insistently at her labia; felt her heart open towards him as finally he moved forwards and into her with his engorged prick.

'I love you,' he murmured as that first thrust brought his face next to Cherry's again. But still he wouldn't let her go, wouldn't run the risk of her unmasking him.

She sighed ecstatically as the next thrust forced the breath from her body, then cooed with delight as he withdrew ever so slightly before preparing to thrust forward again. It started slowly. The stranger held her tightly at the moment when they were most completely joined. Cherry had never felt so cherished. She loved the feel of his tender lips in the hollow of her neck. She delighted in the encompassing warmth of his arm around her waist, while his other hand held her wrists so gently.

It was as if they were joined together in a celestial dance. It was so perfect. Their bodies corresponded to each other like two ballet dancers in a *pas de deux* they had been practising for the whole of their lives. When Cherry moved, the stranger knew exactly what move to make himself. Their actions never jarred against each other. When their bodies came together, there was no clashing, no crashing; they met like those of two lovers who have known each other through generations of reincarnation. They might have met before as fish, birds, or butterflies. But Cherry knew at once that they had definitely known each other well.

The man continued to hold Cherry's arms pinned above her head as he eased himself into her once again. She closed her eyes to savour the early ripples of her orgasm. It was building inside her already and she knew that it would be a fantastic one. Her entire body tensed in preparation. She felt the familiar warmth flooding through her, a tingle of organic electricity starting at her clitoris, an urgent throbbing beginning to echo the faster beating of her heart.

Cherry wrapped her legs tightly around her lover's back, pulling him towards her. She tried to kiss his neck but found that having her arms pinned above her head prevented her from reaching him. Somehow the frustration only aroused her more.

'Come with me,' she begged him. 'Come with me.'

She could feel his penis swell to capacity inside her but the stranger wouldn't come.

'Come with me,' she pleaded again.

She wanted them to experience this tremendous moment together. She wanted to feel that they were joined on every level. She needed him to come at the same time as her.

Instead, just as she was sure that he wouldn't be able to hold back any longer, the stranger suddenly withdrew his slick penis from her vagina and rolled away. He turned his back to her. Cherry immediately moved to be near him again.

'What's the matter?' she asked, pawing desperately at his shoulder.

The stranger moved to face her. He stroked his hand along the edge of Cherry's jaw.

'It's just not the right time,' he told her. 'Not yet.'

'You're always saying not yet,' she protested. 'How can you hold back?'

He put his finger to her lips again.

'I've waited for you for a long time, Cherry. I can wait a little longer. I need to know that you are entirely mine.'

She stared at him angrily.

'I was. Just then, I was.'

'I mean in every sense,' he said. 'Lie down beside me. Try to sleep.'

Try to sleep? Cherry looked at her lover incredulously. This wasn't supposed to happen. How could she try to sleep when he had left her feeling so incomplete? She stared at the profile of his mask in the darkness. His breathing was deep and slow. Was he really falling asleep?

Cherry sat up and stared down at him. If the stranger fell sleep, she would at least be able to get a good look at his face. When she was convinced that he must have dropped off, she stretched out her hand to untie the black ribbon that held her lover's mask in place. She was nowhere near to unfastening the knot when he reached up and grabbed her hand as though he was plucking a blue-bottle out of the air.

'Not yet,' he said, refusing to let go of her wrist.

Cherry lay down silently. She was determined that she would stay awake until he was so deeply asleep that he didn't catch her out. Absolutely determined.

When Cherry awoke, she was immediately aware that the house was empty. The sound of her breathing echoed back to her as it had done on the first occasion that she came to the house.

The memory of the evening up until the moment that she had fallen asleep in the stranger's arms came back in fragments. Cherry's hand flew up to her face when she realised that she wasn't wearing her mask any longer. She found it placed carefully and neatly on the dressing table. Beside it was the stranger's mask. The stranger himself had gone.

'Hello?' Cherry called from the landing, hoping that he was still somewhere in the house. 'Is anybody there?'

Her heart leapt into her throat when she heard footsteps in the hallway below her. She held her hand to her mouth as she waited to see her host appear from the shadows. Would she see his real face now? He had been so determined that she wouldn't see what he looked like before they made love. Did that mean he had been hiding something truly terrible from her? Some kind of deformity that he thought she wouldn't be able to stomach?

'I want to see you again,' she called out waveringly when the footsteps did not bring her lover into the dim light of the chandelier. 'I want to see your face. I don't care what you look like. It doesn't matter to me. I just want to know who you really are.'

But her platitudes didn't stop her heart from racing as she waited for a revelation.

'Please?' she tried again. Her voice wobbled. The footsteps grew closer.

'Miss Valentine?'

Cherry leaned further over the banister to see who was calling. 'Yes.'

'Er, you might want to put some clothes on,' said the man who stepped out of the gloom.

It was the driver.

'I think the party's pretty much over,' he said, looking up at her with his hat still hiding his eyes, though not his familiar mocking grin. 'You're here all on your own.'

Cherry moved away from the stair-rail so that he couldn't see her nakedness.

'Is he gone?' she called down.

'He is,' said the driver, knowing instantly who she meant. 'I'll be waiting for you outside.'

She went back into the bedroom and gathered up her discarded clothing. As she climbed into her dress she couldn't help but think wistfully of his hands upon the buttons she fastened. She couldn't believe that he had taken off his mask while she slept, and crept away before she woke up and saw what he had been so careful to hide. Cherry ran her fingers thoughtfully over the golden face that had covered her lover's. Then she picked up her own mask and hurried down the stairs.

She was the last person to leave the house. When she emerged on to the street, looking considerably more dishevelled than when she had arrived at the party, she could see no car. She was just starting to walk down the road again when the limousine slid around the corner. This time Cherry didn't protest. The driver opened the door using the catch inside the car and she slid inside.

'Who is he?' she asked the driver straightaway.

'I can't tell you that,' he persisted.

'You must tell me,' Cherry insisted, getting out her purse and waving as much money as she had with her through the partition that separated them. 'I need to know.'

The driver waved her hand away.

'I don't want your money,' he told her.

'And I don't want to be made to look an idiot by some freak who insists on wearing a mask to make love to me.'

The driver didn't say another word for the rest of

the journey. When she got out of the car outside her flat, Cherry slammed the door of the limousine shut behind her as if to underline her anger at his silence. The driver didn't react, of course, and the car slipped off into the night.

Cherry went straight to her bedroom and threw herself down on the unmade bed. She felt angry and confused. Even used. She wasn't used to being left in limbo.

But she still had the mask and the single comforting thought that it was so unusual that perhaps it might be easy to trace who had bought it for her. Since Eddie had put her on to the story in the first place, he would be happy to let her divert office resources into the search. She would find out who her masked man was whether he told her himself or not.

'No one makes a fool of me,' she told her reflection in the dressing-table mirror.

It was while Cherry was plotting her revenge that she noticed the little red light on her answer-machine was flashing. She flew across the room to press the button. Perhaps he had called.

'Cherry, are you there? Are you screening your calls? It's Steve. I wondered if I could come round. I just can't sleep without you.'

Cherry groaned.

# Chapter Eight

*EDDIE WASN'T IN* the office when Cherry arrived the next morning. She was relieved that she wouldn't have to give him her version of the night's events yet. She hadn't been able to get much sleep. Her thoughts kept drifting back to what the stranger had said when he first entered her on the ocean-wide four poster bed. He had told her that he loved her. He said that he wanted her to be entirely his. But who was he?

She tried to tell herself that he was obviously just a nutter, that she was better off without his mysterious house-guests and masquerades. But she couldn't stop thinking about him. When she reached her hand up to scratch the back of her neck, she imagined his hand in its place. When she tapped a pencil against her lip as she worked, she imagined his lips touching gently against hers. When she crossed her legs, the pressure on her clitoris made her think of his tongue, his penis. Who was he?

'I'm going mad,' she muttered.

She was almost grateful for the distraction when

Steve came into the office, though his presence only reminded her that she would have to let him down at some point that day.

'It was incredible,' Steve said, unable to temper his observations of the Andreas Eros show with anything as grubby as cynicism. 'I thought it was going to be rubbish. I mean, I've never really liked magicians before. They're all crappier versions of Paul Daniels, as if he wasn't bad enough to begin with. But this was really different.'

'Do tell me,' sighed Cherry, sure that no amount of SFX trickery could quite match the magic she had been part of the previous night.

'Well, to start off with, there seemed to be hundreds of people on the stage. Solid people.'

'People generally are solid,' said Cherry sarcastically.

'No, listen. I was sitting just three rows back from the front and they looked really solid to me. You couldn't have put a hand through their bodies. But then Eros came on stage dressed like something out of *Highlander*, with this massive sword, and started slashing it about, knocking heads off left, right and centre. Some of the people in the audience were screaming. All of the people on the stage were screaming. The American woman sitting next to me was begging her husband to call the police on his mobile. It was as if Eros had gone mad and was killing all his dancers. It was so real,' Steve insisted.

'He does react quite badly to the odd unkind review,' Cherry sneered.

'But then they just disappeared. All the bodies on

the stage disappeared as if they were fading from view like people in an old photograph. It was five minutes before the people at the back of the audience stopped crying. I kept having to check myself for blood. It was so realistic, Cherry. It was the best thing I've ever seen.'

'Amazing what you can do with a projector,' she said flatly. 'Did he do any real tricks?'

'Real tricks? Well, he made an entire stage full of people disappear.'

'You mean he had someone backstage turn a projector off. Steve, I've worked with magicians, I know how they do these things.'

Steve looked at her incredulously. 'When did you work with a magician?'

'A long time ago. I was just out of school. But it certainly opened my eyes to what you can get the general public to believe in. Turn the lights down and the music up and people will believe black is white if they want to.'

'I'm not that stupid,' he said.

'Everyone's that stupid,' Cherry assured him. 'It's all about creating the right atmosphere.'

'So you weren't joking about that hypnotism thing,' he murmured. 'You really did put a spell on your driving instructor.'

'It wasn't a spell, Steve. Just a prime example of what I'm trying to explain to you. Hypnotism is another kind of illusion. It's about making people think they're not in control of their own actions. It's about giving people permission to do the things that common sense or manners stop them from doing anyway. You can't make someone do what they don't want to do. If someone acts like a chicken on stage, it's because they have secret exhibitionist tendencies. My driving instructor secretly wanted to pass me in spite of my three point turns because he thought I might shag him if he did. Now, back to Eros. Did he do anything with cards?'

'No.' Steve was still dumbfounded by the hypnotism thing.

'But he dressed up as a character from *Highlander*?'

'Yes.'

'OK. I think I've got the idea. Take this down. Remember *Highlander*? That twentieth-century film in which a French guy played a Scots man with an Irish accent and Sean Connery played a Spaniard with an accent straight out of Edinburgh? Well, in his new show, Andreas Eros has managed to create something almost as *realistic* . . . Italics for that last word.'

'But it *was* realistic,' Steve protested.

Cherry just squeezed him on the knee and weakened him with a smile.

'I'm sure it was. But nobody expects me to write anything nice about Andreas Eros in my column, do they? If I start now, they'll think that the paper is running scared, and before you know it we won't be allowed to write a bad word about anyone.'

'But you didn't even see the show.'

'Are you going to tell anybody?' Cherry asked.

'No,' he said, smiling sweetly. 'At least, not if you keep me happy,' he added.

'Are you trying to blackmail me?'

'I'd much rather try to ball you.'

Cherry bit her lip and looked nervously about her to see if anyone was listening. 'We've got to be discreet, you know. Employers don't like it when two people in their office start to have an affair. It makes them think of conspiracies.'

'Are we conspiring?' Steve asked.

'Sort of.'

Steve moved towards her and tried to plant a kiss on her cheek.

Cherry jerked her face back out of his range.

'Will you never learn?' she asked him. 'You can't kiss me in the office, you fool. Why don't you go to the conference room on the third floor and see if there's anyone in there.'

'There won't be. It's being decorated.'

'Well, go and see if the decorators are in there. I haven't seen anybody in overalls knocking about. If you're not back here in five minutes, I'll come and join you.'

Steve leapt to his feet eagerly. 'Make that three minutes,' he said.

'OK. Three minutes.'

Cherry watched as he practically ran to the lift. She smoothed her hair back from her face and sighed. What was she doing? She was supposed to be ending things with Steve, not giving in to him once more. She blamed the previous evening's events. If that man hadn't left her feeling so frustrated, perhaps she would be able to keep her hands off the work experience boy.

She remonstrated with herself for letting her clitoris take the lead, but there was no denying the pull of her hormones. She had liked to think herself immune to the forces of nature, but now she knew what it was like to see a perfect body and be unable to stop oneself from wanting to touch it. More than that, from wanting to taste it and have bits of it rubbing up against you.

'I think I may be turning into a dirty old woman,' she told herself, as, a whole minute before the agreed period of time had elapsed, she put the lid back on her pen and headed for the lift in hot pursuit.

When she reached the conference room, Steve was nowhere to be seen. Cherry was about to go back downstairs seething with frustration when he stepped out from a cupboard dressed in nothing but a dust sheet.

'What's this?' she asked. 'A toga party?'

'Invitation only,' said Steve.

'You're mad. What if someone comes in and finds you dressed in nothing but a dust sheet?'

'I'll tell them you made me do it,' he replied, reaching out to drag Cherry towards him by the belt on her skirt.

'You're insatiable,' she murmured, sliding her hand beneath the folds of his toga and seeking out his already erect penis.

'Only with you,' he replied, planting a kiss on her mouth.

Cherry let her head roll backwards as Steve kissed his way down her neck. But fantastic as the sensation of his mouth on her throat was, she couldn't seem to concentrate. Each time she closed her eyes, it wasn't Steve but the man in the golden mask that she imagined making love to her. Whenever she opened her eyes, she was disappointed to see Steve's puppyish grin. He was beautiful. But he wasn't the one she wanted.

She was almost glad when she thought she heard the sound of the lift doors swooshing open on the otherwise deserted floor.

She quietly extricated herself from Steve's embrace and put a finger to her lips as she listened out to see if she had been right. A peculiar dragging sound was approaching them. Steve was wide-eyed as he tried to comprehend what she had already guessed.

'In here, Jim,' the first decorator said, barging open the door with his backside so that he could carry a painting table in. Thinking quickly, Cherry shoved Steve backwards into a tall metal filing cabinet and threw his discarded clothes in after him. She just about managed to straighten herself up before the decorators managed to negotiate the narrow doorway and discovered that they were not alone.

'You can't use this room, love,' said the one called Jim. 'We've come to give it a paint job.'

'I know,' said Cherry, smoothing down her hair. 'I was just looking for some files.'

'Nothing in here. It was all cleared out last week,' said Jim.

'I know that now,' she said. 'I'll leave you to get on with your work.'

She slipped out into the corridor, barely able to control her giggles. Poor Steve, left there in the filing cabinet. Inside the room, the decorators were setting up their table, opening paint pots and getting ready for a hard day's work. Cherry hoped for Steve's sake that they were typical of their trade and stopped for a coffee break as soon as they were set up. But that was his problem. In the meantime, she wasn't going to hang about. It was lunchtime and all that frustration had made her very hungry.

'I want to see that witch!'

When Cherry came back from lunch the office was a war zone. Two security staff were hovering by the door, ready to spring into action as soon as Eddie gave the nod. He was keeping a desk safely between himself and his visitor.

Andreas Eros.

Cherry fancied that she could smell his heady aftershave even before the lift door opened on to the editorial floor. Eddie caught her eye and frantically gestured her back into the lift, but he wasn't frantic enough. Either that or Cherry was ready for a fight, because she stepped straight into his office, smiling warmly at the magician she had just annihilated with words, once again.

'What do you mean by this?' asked Andreas, brandishing the page he had ripped out of the first edition of that evening's paper in her face.

'Oh, the Dixons sale,' Cherry said lightly, deliberately reading from an advert on the wrong side of the page. 'Are you going to buy yourself a new sound system for your show?'

Eddie couldn't surpress a smirk.

'I don't know why you find it all so funny,' Andreas snarled at him. 'You're going to be hearing from my lawyers. I think the court might have something to say about such an unfair review written by a journalist who didn't even have the decency to turn up to the show she was so intent on slagging.'

'How could she have written the review if she didn't turn up?' asked Eddie.

'You tell me,' Andreas replied, folding his arms across his chest and leaning back defensively.

'Of course I was there,' said Cherry, careful not to look anyone in the eye in case she couldn't fight the urge to explode into laughter. 'I took Steve, didn't I?'

'The work experience boy,' Andreas snorted. 'I know all about him. And my assistant saw him sitting on his own in the front row.'

'Were you spying on me?' asked Cherry indignantly.

'I wanted to make sure you were in your seat so that I could present you with a bunch of orchids that I had had flown in specially from Amsterdam.'

'Ah, sweet. But I think that would have been bribery,' she said flatly.

'I demand an apology.'

Eddie looked to Cherry expectantly, no doubt praying that she would see her way clear to uttering just a couple of words that might placate him. Eddie wasn't entirely convinced that Eros was the type who would really sue, but he couldn't be sure. He certainly had the money to hire a damn good lawyer. A stellar-successful season in Las Vegas had made Eros one of the most highly paid entertainers in the world.

Cherry took her time. She drank Eros's agitated appearance in, from his angrily tapping left foot in its gleaming patent shoe, to the showy splash of the fake red amaryllis in his buttonhole. If he hadn't been such an arsehole, she could almost have fancied him.

'I'm sorry I didn't make it to your show,' she said finally.

Eddie breathed an audible sigh of relief, but Andreas Eros's stony expression only got stonier.

'That wasn't quite the apology I had in mind.'

'Well, if you're expecting me to apologise for the article I wrote, you've got a long wait ahead of you. From Steve's description of the show, I'd say it sounded pretty bloody ropey and that's what I wrote. Dressing up in a kilt and lopping people's heads off? C'mon. Steve said that people in the audience were screaming and retching with fear. What kind of entertainment is that?'

'I had a standing ovation.'

'In front of your mirror every night, I'm sure.'

'Don't you believe in my ability to create real magic?' Eros asked suddenly.

Eddie looked at Cherry nervously as she considered the question. What was he hoping to hear? Cherry held Eros's gaze and stared back at him while her lips curled upwards in amusement.

'Real magic? I don't know what you're talking about. Excuse me, Mr Eros, but I've got a real story to file.'

And with that, she turned and flounced in the direction of her desk. Then she walked straight past it and out on to the fire escape for a much-needed cigarette.

Though she had been cool as a cucumber in Eddie's office, Cherry's heart was pounding as if it might burst through her ribcage at any moment. She had hoped that by facing Eros off like that she might have deterred him from the idea of suing, but now she was seriously considering the possibility that she had just made the most stupid move of her career.

She didn't feel any better about the whole affair when Eddie joined her on the fire escape, lighting up a cigarette even as he stepped out on to the rickety iron staircase.

'Fucking hell, Cherry,' he muttered.

They both looked down to see a sleek black limousine draw up alongside the back door of the paper's offices. For a second, Cherry's heart was in her mouth. Was it *the* car? The car that always turned up to take her to the white house? But then she saw the top of Andreas Eros's coiffeured head as he swept out through the back door, throwing his black cape around him like Dracula going home after a good night out. It was his car. And in any case, black limousines were ten a penny in Central London.

'I could spit on him from here,' Cherry told her boss.

'I would really rather you didn't,' said Eddie dryly. 'Jeez, I thought he was never going to go. What did you have to go and write something like that for, Cherry?'

'You're the editor. You could have done some editing.'

'You know that I always play golf on a Wednesday afternoon. I have to be able to trust my staff not to bring libel suits raining down upon us in my absence.'

'He won't sue,' said Cherry, sounding much more confident than she actually felt.

'Well, it's coming out of your wages if he does. I'm only taking this as calmly as I am because I know that you're about to assure me that the story you were chasing up when you should have been watching his poxy show is going to give me the biggest front page of the freakin' millennium. Where have you been lately, Cherry?'

'What do you mean where have I been? You sent me to that party last night.'

'What party?' Eddie looked blank.

'The one you called me about,' said Cherry, becoming agitated. 'The limousine. The masked ball? Remember?'

Eddie still looked blank. 'Did I call you last night?' he asked.

Cherry nodded.

'Jeez. I must have had more to drink than I thought. I can't remember a thing. Perhaps my mind's been wiped clean by Eros's hypnotism tape. When the one I bought didn't seem to be working, he recorded me a personal one. Made me feel a bit strange.' Eddie laughed a little nervously.

Cherry looked at him doubtfully for a moment. 'I'd stick with the Jim Beam theory in public, Ed.'

'I don't know what you've got against that Eros bloke anyway,' he said, recovering himself. 'He wears some poncey clothes and all that, but I'm sure he's all right underneath. He's just an ordinary bloke who's done well by dressing like a vampire and making ladies faint. Lots of women like it. If he sues, it could bankrupt the paper. Why d'you have to go to such great lengths to get his back up, Cherry?'

Watching the limousine pull around the corner, she shrugged dismissively. 'I really don't know.'

'Well, I wish you'd at least try to like him. Just a little bit,' Eddie sighed. 'It doesn't hurt to say flattering things about people with lots of money from time to time. Now, where's young Steve been all afternoon, that's what I want to know. I haven't seen him since the meeting this morning. Has he taken the day off or something?'

'Steve? I think he might be doing some research into claustrophobia,' said Cherry, biting her lip to restrain a smile.

Just at that moment Steve appeared, blushing and dishevelled, from the lift.

'Where've you been, you slacker?' shouted Eddie, climbing back into the office. 'I had to fetch my own lunch today. That's your job.'

'I'm sorry, Eddie,' Steve blustered. 'You'll never believe it but I managed to get myself stuck in a filing cabinet. I was looking for a file. I stepped into the cupboard and the door must have closed behind me. It took ages until someone came along to let me out.'

Eddie looked at him sceptically.

'You stepped *into* the cabinet? You're weird, lad, you know that?'

Cherry gave Steve a sly wink in passing.

'Terribly sorry about that,' she smiled.

When she got back to her desk, Cherry discovered that the post boy had done his rounds. Her eyes alighted at once on the envelope addressed in a familiar swirly hand. Picking it from the pile of competition entries and letters of vitriol from women who thought that Andreas Eros was a god and Cherry should be shot for thinking otherwise, she took the letter from her new mystery lover with her to the ladies room.

Safely inside a cubicle, she closed the lid of the toilet and sat upon it as she turned the envelope over in her hand, unsure what she wanted to find inside. Would this be the moment when she got an explanation? Would he ask to see her again? Cherry felt almost sick as she edged her fingertip beneath the envelope's sharp flap. Funny to think that less than twenty-four hours earlier she had been sitting on her kitchen windowsill, wondering if anyone would ever truly move her again. Now it had happened. But she wasn't sure if she was in love or afraid. Could she possibly have fallen for someone she knew so little about? Did she *want* to see him again?

He certainly wanted to see her. And he would send the car again that evening. Late. So late. Cherry sighed in frustration when she looked at her watch and realised that almost another ten hours would have to pass before she could see her lover again. What would she do until then?

As it happened, Cherry had some pressing business to deal with first.

Steve had left the office before her, but she wasn't surprised to find him sitting on the steps that led to the entrance of her mansion block when she got home.

'I brought you some supper,' he told her, brandishing a carrier bag full of goodies. There was also a good bottle of wine, Cherry duly noted when she took it from him. 'You don't mind me coming over, do you?' he asked as she poured them both a glass.

'No, of course I don't,' she told him. 'In fact, there's something we should talk about tonight anyway.'

She thought she saw a look of fleeting panic zip across his blue eyes. Cherry knew well that most men assumed that, when a woman says she wants to talk, they are going to get the equally unwelcome news of an unplanned pregnancy or a demand for an engagement ring. Not many of them would consider the possibility that they were about to be dumped. Oh no. But if Steve thought any of these terrible things were coming, he didn't betray his fears beyond that initial spark of worry.

'Great,' he said with a pretty convincing smile. 'Shall we eat first?'

Cherry nodded and he started to unpack the goodies. Perhaps letting him cook first wasn't entirely fair, but she was very hungry and the time it took him to prepare her supper would give her time to prepare her speech.

'What are you making?' she asked him.

'I can only make one thing. I'm afraid it's going to be stir-fry. But I've got chocolate mousse for afters.' He grinned naughtily. Cherry grinned back. Stir-fry? She could take it or leave it. But chocolate mousse?

'Perhaps we should just start with the mousse,' she said, thinking, If we skip straight to dessert we can get this whole thing over with more quickly.

Steve dropped the vegetable knife immediately and, leaving a half-peeled carrot on the table top, he hurried to the fridge where the mousse was waiting. It was a big tub. Family size. He pulled away the lid to reveal a smooth, cocoa powder dusted surface that looked as welcoming to Cherry as the blue water of a hotel swimming pool at the end of a hot dusty day on the road.

She fetched a spoon from the cutlery draw and wistfully ran its cool shiny back along Steve's cheek before she dug it into the surface of the mousse and gouged out a perfect hole. She took a delicate little lick of her spoon before she offered the rest to him.

'Delicious,' she murmured as he licked the spoon clean. 'Thanks for getting it.'

'Shall we divide it into bowls?' Steve asked.

'Why make extra washing up?' she said.

Steve's eyes flashed and Cherry realised that he didn't think she was inviting him to eat the mousse straight from the tub.

'Steve, I didn't mean . . .' she began.

'Sit on the table,' he suggested.

She shook her head in a feeble gesture of dissent, but before she knew it she was sitting on the cold Formica table top and Steve was unbuttoning her blouse.

'Steve, we need to . . .' she started, as he placed a kiss on her breast-bone, where her silken slip dipped into a sexy V.

Soon she was completely naked again. Steve gently pushed her back until she was lying flat out on the table, then he loaded the spoon with mousse and blobbed a line of the delicious stuff all the way from her collar-bone to her pubis.

'Steve,' Cherry murmured, but there was less

protest in her voice now. Fixing his wicked eyes on hers, Steve dipped his head and poked out his long tongue. Cherry shivered when he licked up a mouthful of mousse from just above her belly-button. This was undoubtedly going to make it much harder to say what she needed to say to him, but... Cherry defied anyone to resist temptation in the form of a firm young guy with a bowlful of mousse at his disposal.

Steve planted a kiss on her lips before he moved down her body again. This time he hesitated level with her waist, first gently tracing the outline of her navel with his tongue, then probing at it, penetrating it, until she began to squirm. Down below his kisses, Cherry could already feel herself becoming aroused, in spite of her best intentions to do otherwise.

Her cunt grew wetter and warmer as Steve slurped up the last of the mousse and drenched her belly-button with saliva. After a while, she had to push him away to persuade him to concentrate on the areas that mattered more.

He pulled a chair up to the kitchen table and parted Cherry's legs so that she lay fully exposed to him. Teasingly, he picked up her legs and began to lick at her slender ankles. Then he moved on to her toes. Sucking a little toe between his teeth, he told her that he didn't need the mousse as Cherry's naked skin was the sweetest thing he had ever tasted.

'Don't tease me,' she begged him.

'After what you did to me today? Locking me in that filing cabinet?'

'I'm sorry,' she protested. 'I didn't mean that to happen, I swear.'

'Were you left feeling as frustrated as I was?'

Without waiting for an answer, Steve slid his hands up Cherry's smooth calves, following close behind them with his mouth, and kissing a damp chocolate-smeared path along the inside of her legs until his hot lips reached the tops of her thighs. She clutched the edges of the table as Steve finally nuzzled his gorgeous face against the soft triangle of her pubic hair.

His agile tongue quickly found her clitoris, which was already swollen from the anticipation of his attention. Already knowing what she liked best, Steve used his tongue to flick the tiny button of desire from side to side until it was hard enough for him to suck it between his plump lips like a miniature penis. Cherry breathed in sharply when he gave her the gentlest of nips. She gasped, not from pain but from exquisite pleasure. How could she contemplate letting this man go?

But when he slipped his hands between her thighs again, it wasn't Steve's face that filled her mind. When he parted her labia with his careful fingers, Cherry was thinking of the cold touch of the stranger's mask on her skin as he laid his head against her flat stomach. Her vulva was already slick with the juice of her desire, but it wasn't for Steve that her body prepared itself.

Oblivious to the fact that Cherry's mind was with another lover, Steve caressed the smooth pink lips of her vulva with his mouth. The warm musky scent of her awakening body provided a heady counterpoint to the smell of the chocolate. Steve wanted nothing so much as to eat Cherry then. He nipped her thigh, unable to resist the temptation of her smooth, pale skin. Cherry felt her body reach that point beyond which she could not accept that she might be left unfulfilled.

'Take me, please,' she begged, imagining not Steve, as he pulled her towards the edge of the table, but the stranger.

Positioning himself between Cherry's legs, Steve slid his hand down between their bodies and guided his eager, solid penis between her legs. Cherry gasped as if she was surprised by the first thrust, but quickly relaxed again when she felt his pelvis make the connection with hers. But she still wasn't thinking of Steve. In her mind, she was not lying on the kitchen table, but on the four poster bed.

She kept her eyes tightly shut against Steve's gaze as he began to move. If she opened her eyes and allowed herself to see him for even a moment, the illusion would be finished. With her eyes closed, Cherry could see the stranger looming above her. She could see the muscles of his arms tightening as he supported his weight upon them. She could see his abdominal muscles separating into six perfect symmetrical bands as he thrust his penis forward into her body.

Cherry reached up to run her hands across Steve's chest, imagining all the time that he was someone else. Steve, unknowing, sighed with pleasure as her fingers trailed lightly down his body. He threw his head back when she tucked her hands behind him and took hold of his buttocks, not thinking for a second that her mind was not with him.

It wasn't long before Steve came. Cherry sensed

the moment he lost control. She felt his penis jerk upwards against the roof of her vagina, her g-spot, as it prepared itself for the final thrust.

Her own climax came quietly, almost apologetically, as if the whole of her body knew that this would be the last time she allowed Steve to make love with her.

When she opened her eyes, Steve was smiling down at her. She waited until he had pulled out of her body, then sat up hurriedly. She jumped from the table and snatched up her blouse.

Steve noticed immediately that something was different.

'Are you OK?' he asked.

'Fine,' Cherry said, between sips from a large glass of wine. 'I'm fine. Come through here.'

She led him into the sitting room. Steve sat down beside her, still smiling, his eyes wide and soft like a puppy's. Cherry reached up and stroked his face. He was so, so sweet. It was a pity sweet wasn't what she wanted. How easy life would be, she mused, if everyone wanted the people who wanted them back.

'You said that you had something to say to me,' he ventured. 'Is now a good time to talk?'

When would there ever be a good time? Cherry knew that every time she let Steve into her home (or into the book cupboard) that she would simply have to let him make love to her. But she also knew that every time she let him make love to her, she was strengthening his belief that there was more between them than a mad, passionate meeting of bodies. She pulled her shirt more tightly around her to retain some of the warmth that the latest bout of love-making had generated.

'Is it good news?' he asked.

'Sort of. You've finished your apprenticeship, Steve,' she told him.

'What?' He clearly didn't understand.

'I said you've finished your apprenticeship,' she murmured. 'I don't want you to come round here anymore.'

'What?' he said again. 'What do you mean? Are you dumping me, Cherry? You can't dump me. We just . . .'

Cherry put a finger to his lips.

'I'm not dumping you, Steve. Not exactly. I'm just letting you go so that you can move on to better things.'

'I don't know what you're talking about,' he said. His face wore the twisted expression of an actor in a television drama who has just been told that his son is a murderer, or his sister is dead. He looked unbelieving. Hostile. He wanted to be told it wasn't true. 'Don't do this to me, Cherry,' he begged. 'I want to be with you. I want to be your boyfriend.'

'No, you don't,' she smiled. 'You just wanted to be with me because I seemed glamorous to you.'

'Don't patronise me,' he warned.

'I'm not. I'm just telling it as it is. I've been there, remember. Power's an aphrodisiac. I've got more power than you, so you fancy me. You wouldn't have looked twice at me if our situations were reversed.'

'It isn't true,' he shook his head.

'You'll see that it is. We could never have worked

as an item, Steve. It's not just because of the office or the age difference. I'm not looking for a relationship right now and I don't think you are either. You could have anybody you want. Why don't you have a few more before you start talking about settling down.'

Steve leapt up from the sofa and started to look for his clothes. 'You don't know what you're doing, Cherry. If you think you can treat someone this shabbily and get away with it, you had better start writing your CV. I know more about you than anyone else in the office, and I don't just mean where your birthmarks are.'

Cherry smiled. 'Don't say such things, Steve. Blackmail is very ugly.'

'So, now you're getting a taste of your own medicine. You get half your stories by blackmailing people with threats that you'll write something worse about them if they don't give you what you want.'

'That's the business we're in.'

'Well, let's see how happy you are when I talk to Eddie about a little bit of business that's gone on between us.'

'No point.'

Steve paused in the middle of tying up a shoe. He looked at Cherry with eyes full of hatred.

'I've already talked to him. I spoke to Eddie this afternoon and told him that it was you who got the Madonna story and then I admitted that I did send you to the Andreas Eros show alone.'

'And he didn't sack you?'

'No, he didn't. But I did help him to make up his mind about one thing.'

Steve looked at her expectantly.

Cherry reached into the handbag she had flung down in the corner of her bedroom and pulled out an envelope. 'I thought you'd like to have this this evening. Eddie was going to put it in the post.'

Steve took the envelope warily and ripped it open. Cherry watched his face, knowing how he would react. As soon as he reached the second paragraph, the angry, thunderous expression that had been marking his beautiful face was replaced by the smile that had never failed to charm Cherry's knickers off. Eddie had offered him a permanent job on the paper.

When he had finished reading the letter, Steve immediately read it through again just to be sure he wasn't dreaming, and only then did he allow himself to punch the air. 'I got a job,' he told Cherry, as if she didn't know.

'Congratulations. Just don't forget who gave you a good reference,' she joked as she ambled towards the shower.

By the time she had finished soaping herself down, Steve had gone. She found a note on her dressing-table, written, she noticed with just a little annoyance, in her favourite eye-liner pencil.

'No hard feelings. See you in the office. <u>My</u> office too now.'

She crumpled the note and tossed it into the waste paper bin with a sigh of relief. That had gone reasonably well. And she still had an hour left to get ready for the main business of the evening. She had been dreading having to push Steve out the door with the matter of their 'relationship' still unresolved. Now she could relax once more and take time to make sure that she looked her best for that night's more important show-down.

# Chapter Nine

*CHERRY WAITED IN* the dark for the car to arrive again. She couldn't remember the last time she had taken so much care to prepare herself for an assignation. Following her hurried shower, designed merely as an opportunity to make herself scarce while Steve gathered his belongings and left the house, she had run herself a deep, hot bath. She had anointed her body with perfumed oil, smoothed her skin, and softened her shining hair. She outlined her brown eyes with jet black pencil that made them look large and luminous. Her lips were painted blood-red, like the kissable petals of a dangerous flower.

The confusion of her feelings towards the stranger still eddied about in her mind like occasional swirls of mud in an otherwise clear pool. She wondered if she was simply making a fool of herself by going along with his game. But she knew that if she didn't return to the house at least one more time; if she didn't try to force her host to reveal his identity to her, she wouldn't be free of the thoughts that had haunted her since she first stepped through his door.

Though their love-making hadn't reached what she would have called a satisfying conclusion, Cherry had been shocked by the height of arousal she had reached in the stranger's arms. It was as though she had been given the tiniest amount of an incredibly addictive drug. Now she couldn't get him out of her mind. It felt as though the only thing that would clear her head was a larger dose of the thing that had muddied her thoughts in the first place. Was she experiencing the moment she had hoped for? Were these the giddy feelings of falling in love?

When the car arrived, Cherry looked down on its sleek black lines from the dark safety of her flat and gave herself one more chance to stop this craziness. With the lights out, she could pretend that she wasn't at home. The driver would go away and the mystery would be over. Albeit unresolved.

The driver walked up to the house, hat still over his eyes. He leaned against the doorframe and pressed the buzzer so that it seemed to play a little tune.

Cherry took a deep breath and opened the door.

'Are you ready?' he asked, all wolfish grin. For a second Cherry found herself thinking how kissable *his* mouth looked. She felt so much anticipation. So much arousal.

She nodded and followed the driver out to the car. This time, she didn't press him to find out who his employer was. She knew that was pointless. Instead, she gazed out of the car window, deep in thought, and didn't even notice when the limousine finally pulled into the road where the white house stood.

Once again, it was empty. No music. No staff. No sign of a party that night. Cherry waited in the echoing hallway. A bubble of anticipation, a mixture of excitement and inexplicable fear, lodged in her throat, making it difficult for her to breathe. She put her hand to her neck in an attempt to calm herself. So much time seemed to pass as she stood there alone. The only sounds in the house were those she made herself. She was almost ready to give up and leave when the door to the cellar creaked open as slowly as it had done on the night when Cherry was sure she had come face to face with a leopard.

This time, she knew the form. Though the evocative sound of that unoiled door couldn't help but raise her heartbeat just a little as she recalled other evenings, she stepped down into the cellar. A thousand candles warmed the dusty air. The stage had been dismantled again. Cherry walked slowly to the foot of the bed where her masked lover lay naked on the pillows.

'You came back,' he said, smiling beneath the golden eye-piece. 'I knew that you would.'

Cherry nodded. The stranger patted the surface of the bed beside him and invited her to sit down.

'You left me in the middle of the night,' she reminded him.

'You looked so lovely as you slept,' he said, caressing her unmasked face. 'I didn't want to wake you.'

'But you took your mask off.'

'I'll take it off again tonight,' he promised.

'When?' she pleaded.

He answered her with a kiss.

'Just trust me,' he said to her. 'You can wait a little longer.'

She shook her head, but allowed herself to melt into the stranger's arms. She allowed him to unbutton the pale blue dress she had chosen for this meeting, and to kiss her naked skin, softened and smoothed by her bath. She allowed him to stroke her into submission once more.

In the soft candlelight, the man's body looked even more beautiful than she remembered. She ran her hands wonderingly over his wide shoulders, traced the outline of his square pectoral muscles, and planted reverent kisses on each of his nipples. The stranger rolled over on to his back so that his penis reached up into the air magnificently. Cherry knelt beside her lover and bent her head until her lips touched the glistening head of his shaft. She wanted to taste him as well as touch him. She wanted him so much.

'What is it about you?' she murmured.

'Don't you think it's possible that we were made for each other?' he asked her. 'Look at how well our bodies fit together. We're like two halves of the same strange fruit.' He pulled her to lie down beside him again so that the swell of her hip fitted the curve of his waist. Then he rolled on top of her and straddled her, resting his smooth chin between her breasts. Cherry felt the tip of his penis touch her thigh. His breath upon her naked skin raised goosebumps.

He lifted his head and smiled at her. Deep in Cherry's subconscious, a tiny flicker of recognition glittered and then died before she could catch it.

'Isn't it as though we've known each other for a long time?' she commented, hoping to recapture the glimmer again when he reacted.

'A long time,' he agreed. But Cherry was left unsure whether he meant that they had known each other in a real tangible sense or whether they had met at a party, or in a gallery, or at a bus stop. Or in another life.

'When did we meet?' she tried.

'Do you mean to say you don't remember?'

He kissed his way down her body, then parted her legs and knelt between them. Still smiling at her lovingly, he slid his warm hand towards the entrance to her vagina. It felt like an age until his finger finally breached her labia and touched her inside. She allowed her hips to buck upwards, pushing his finger deeper as she moved. She wanted to be penetrated by him. She realised that she had wanted him without a moment's pause in her desire since he had left her lying alone on the four poster bed the night before.

'I don't know why I think I can trust you,' she murmured again. 'But I just felt compelled to be with you. I would have walked naked across London just to be here tonight. Did you feel the same?'

'Drawn together as if by magic,' the stranger agreed, a small smile playing over his lips as he thrust his fingers inside her again and revelled in the sight of Cherry throwing her head back in a gesture of delight.

'I want you,' she told him. 'I want you inside me every night. I want to be yours.'

The stranger pushed his fingers a little deeper.

'Not just your hand,' she told him, reaching towards where his penis bobbed upwards. 'I want you inside me totally. And I want you to come with me when I come.'

Cherry wrapped her hand around his shaft and started to manipulate his erection. His smile contorted into an expression of quiet ecstasy as blood flooded through his veins. It wasn't long before he climbed on top of her again and helped her to guide his penis between her longing labia.

'Don't leave me wanting you this time,' she begged him. 'I want this to be perfect.'

Cherry let her eyes drift to the place where their pelvises met, to the way he was thrusting slowly in and out of her so that their bodies appeared like two parts of the same fantastically well-oiled machine. The sight of the stranger's glistening dick plunging into her was almost as good as the feeling it gave her deep inside. She felt her vagina begin to pulse in appreciation of him with the very first stroke. It was a steady, rhythmic pulse that began to spread slowly throughout her limbs like the insistent heat of the spring sun melting ice.

He knew exactly what Cherry wanted. She had a peculiar sense that he always had done. When he was sure that she was almost unbearably aroused, he began to change the direction and depth of his thrusts. Whether he was aiming straight for her g-spot or just tickling at the edges of her labia with the very tip of his throbbing shaft, each and every stroke was carefully calculated to drive her closer to the moment of ultimate release.

Cherry lifted her legs from the bed and wound them tightly around the stranger's body, at the same time grasping his buttocks with her hands and using them to bring him further inside her still. Her fingers dug hard into his soft warm flesh as she grew more and more excited, forcing him to increase the pace of his movement to keep time with her racing breath.

This time she was not going to let him go until he came inside her. She would not be satisfied if he allowed her to reach the point of orgasm alone. Tonight, however, that didn't seem likely to happen. With Cherry's finely muscled thighs holding him tight against her body, the stranger pumped his pelvis more and more frantically. It wasn't long before it became apparent that he was no longer in control of both their desires.

This time, when she cried out for him to come with her, her ecstatic plea was answered. Cherry opened her eyes wide with surprise when she felt the familiar signal of his penis pressing up against her g-spot. His mouth was open, as if he too had been overtaken by the unexpected. Their bodies were suddenly pulled hard against each other as if by some invisible emotional force. Cherry's vagina began to throb and contract in perfect harmony with the pumping of his penis. Perfect harmony. It was the ultimate shared moment.

Cherry was left clinging tightly to her lover's body like a sailor washed overboard. She couldn't bear to let him go when the orgasm was over. And from the way he clung tightly to her, it seemed that the feeling was returned.

Eventually, he eased himself up on to his elbows to look down into her face. Cherry knew that at that moment she looked her most beautiful. She knew that her eyes would be deep and dark, her lips full and red, her cheeks flushed. She knew that the stranger could see her heart in her face. He had seen everything there was to know about Cherry Valentine.

But she still didn't know anything about him.

'I've got to know who you are,' she begged him.

The masked man rolled off her sweating body and backed away from her hands as she reached out to pull his mask away.

'Please,' she begged again. 'You've got to let me see you now. I just know that there could be more to this than just sex.'

She bit her tongue as soon as she said the words. 'More to this than sex.' Was it really Cherry Valentine speaking?

'I think I might be falling in love,' she said with a self-deprecating laugh. 'My head is just full of you. I can't think of anything else. I don't want to think of anything else. But at the same time, you've got to understand, I don't feel like I can really trust you until I know,' she added in a more plaintive voice.

'How do I know I can trust you?' the stranger asked.

'I'll tell you everything there is to know about me,' she tried, sensing, she thought, that he was softening to her demands.

'I already know everything there is to know about you. And that's what makes me think I can't trust you at all, Cherry Valentine.'

'Why not?'

'Why not? Because you've made your living by breeching people's trust. By telling lies. By humiliating people to amuse your audience,' he said.

Cherry started at the anger in his voice. 'But that

is my job. I would never humiliate someone I loved. Never. You've got to let me see you. I think I've fallen in love with you and I feel so foolish falling for someone whose face I've never seen. I don't even know your name.'

'You will do,' he said. 'And I don't think you'll forget who I am in a hurry.'

'I don't ever want to forget,' she said as she finally, joyfully, pulled his mask away.

It took a few seconds before the full horror of the revelation sank in. Cherry's expression of excitement slowly melted away as she took in the black hair, the thick lips, the deep-set eyes that looked as though they had been carved out of coal, and pieced them together to form a face. It was a face that was all too familiar.

'Surprised?' he asked.

Cherry couldn't even bring herself to answer.

'Still think you might be falling in love with me?' asked Andreas Eros.

'It's y— you,' Cherry finally managed to form the words.

'You are surprised,' he laughed. 'But does it change things, Cherry? Does it make the love we made any less good?' He reached out and let a strand of her hair run through his fingers. His smile was wicked, teasing, anything but friendly.

'You tricked me,' she shouted.

'How did I trick you?'

'You didn't tell me who you were.'

'Has anybody you've met in this house ever told you who they really were?' he asked pointedly.

'No. But you knew who I was. You knew that if I'd

known I was about to get into bed with you, I would have run a mile.'

'And wouldn't we both have missed out if you had?'

'Don't try to make me say something like that.' Cherry snarled. She drew the covers around her angrily as he tried to touch her breast. 'It was you who arranged for me to come here in the first place, wasn't it?'

'You got into the car that had been sent for someone else entirely. How was I to know that you were the kind of girl who would deprive someone else of their taxi.'

'There was no other passenger. You knew that I would have to get into that car. There was no other way I could get back from that Godforsaken place, and you tricked me. You've kept me here against my will.'

'Against your will? That's not how it looked to me.'

'That's how it will look in the papers.'

'Really? What exactly will you write, Cherry? What will your readers think if you tell them that you made wonderful love to a man, told him that you had fallen for him and then changed your mind when you found out that it was me? I don't think that's much of a front page story,' he added haughtily. 'In fact, most people will think you've written the piece because you couldn't have me, not because you did.'

Cherry couldn't stop herself. Before she knew what she was doing, she had made one of her elegant hands into a fist and punched Eros right on his aquiline nose. He fell backwards, clutching at his face.

'You can send the plastic surgeon's bill to my solicitor,' she screamed.

# Chapter Ten

*CHERRY STORMED FROM* the house.

How *could* it be him? How could the person who had turned her on more than anyone before possibly be Andreas Eros? He was a horrible little man. A stunted personality who kept his own self-esteem high by making the people around him look pathetic with his silly tricks. He was as creative as a brick. As original as a print of Andy Warhol's *Campbell Soup Can*. How could he possibly have made love to her so wonderfully, so expertly? So softly that she almost wanted to cry at the emotion which emanated from his hands when he touched her.

It can't have been him, Cherry told herself firmly. It was someone who looked very much like him. I didn't ever see my real golden-masked lover's face. Eros must have paid someone else to make love to me before substituting himself once I was hooked.

But she knew that wasn't true. Until he had unveiled himself to her and spoiled his greatest illusion so far, she had been certain that she was making love to the person who had made her feel so special the night before. Everything was ruined.

She went straight to bed when she reached home, and lay tossing and turning on the sheets she hadn't straightened after Steve had left so happily, clutching his first proper job offer. Now she felt that she was the one who had been cheated.

'Did you get your big story?' Steve asked when she met him in the lift the next morning.

'I don't suppose you've got any good Madonna pics you could lend me?' Cherry quipped.

'Not any more,' he replied cockily.

A new work experience intern had already taken Steve's place. Karen, the new girl, was in Eddie's office, listening to his spiel about the role of the tabloid and the freedom of the press. Steve had heard that speech when he first arrived to take up his position on the paper. Cherry had heard it once too.

'Nice arse,' said Steve, nudging Cherry and nodding in the direction of Karen's neat backside as she leaned over Eddie's desk to take a closer look at some negatives.

'Please don't use the book cupboard,' said Cherry, full of mock distress. 'I couldn't bear it if you used our special place.'

But she wasn't really bothered where Steve shagged the new intern. She was bothered by the loss of her other lover. She took herself off to the library on the pretence of writing an article on women writers who advanced their careers by pretending to be men, while really all she wanted to do was wallow in her thoughts. She hadn't slept well. When she closed her eyes she could only see

Eros. The stranger in the mask. Eros. Melting into one another. Because they were the same person. That much she finally had to admit. Especially when she discovered that the amaryllis she had worn to the masked ball had not returned home with her. It was almost certainly the same fake flower that Eros had been wearing in his button-hole when he came into the office to demand an apology for her latest cruel review.

Cherry cringed to think of how clever she had thought herself when she squared up to him that afternoon. All the time he had been mocking her. He had had her stupid hair decoration sticking out of his top pocket for heaven's sake! If he had walked into the library then, she could have torn him limb from limb.

'Why does it have to change things?' he had asked her. Why was the experience they had shared any less special now that she knew who her lover really was? She almost convinced herself that he was right, that she had over-reacted. Then she remembered the triumphant look on his face when she finally got his mask off. He had been so proud of himself for having duped her. That single expression was what had changed things between them.

It didn't help matters that Marie, the features editor, was working on a profile of the bastard and kept shrieking out juicy facts about Eros across the office for everyone, especially Cherry, to hear.

'Remember that supermodel he was engaged to?' she called out. 'Well, she's just given me the most amazing quote. She said that when she met him, it was as if he hypnotised her with his touch. She couldn't bear the sight of him at first. She thought he was an arrogant little dwarf.'

'He's five feet eleven, isn't he?' said Eddie, who was very sensitive to the 'dwarf' word, being only five feet two in his Cuban heels.

'Yeah,' Marie agreed, 'but Marizia Canova is six feet two in her stockings. Anyway, she said that as soon as he touched her, it was as if he had put a spell on her, and suddenly she couldn't think of him as anything other than the most amazing man on earth. It was just like that scene in *A Midsummer Night's Dream* when Titania falls for the Donkey. Maybe you should ask him for some tips, Eddie?'

'If I touched you with my magic wand,' he said bawdily, 'you wouldn't ever look at another man again.' Then he chased Marie round the room with his groin thrust forwards like a satyr. He was fortunate that the *Star Times* office had yet to drag itself into the politically correct twenty-first century with a code on office behaviour that prohibited even the most well-meaning flirt without a written contract first.

Marie and Eddie came to a skidding standstill in front of Cherry's desk.

'What do you think, Cherry?' Marie asked. 'Is Eros an irresistible love god who can mould women like putty with his magical hands? Or is Marizia Canova just another silly cow with more lipstick than sense when it comes to men? I was thinking we could do a for and against article. Marizia could write the "for". Well, I'd probably write that for her, of course, and you could write the "against". Like you usually do.'

Cherry looked horrified by the thought. Could

Marie read her mind? Was she taking the piss? Did she know what had happened?

'I don't think I want to get involved,' she said, in as measured a tone as she could muster. Of course Marie didn't know. Cherry was getting paranoid.

'You would have jumped at the chance to do this last week,' said Marie in surprise.

'Yeah. Well maybe I don't feel qualified to comment any more,' replied Cherry.

'Don't tell me you've been hit by the amazing love-stick too,' said Marie rolling her eyes. 'I guess I'll just have to write both sides of the argument.'

She sauntered back to her desk, with a wink to Eddie over her shoulder as she went. Eddie lingered by Cherry's desk, about to say something.

Cherry scored an angry line through the heart she had been doodling absent-mindedly, and was just expressing her anger even more effectively by scrunching the paper up and imagining that it was Eros's head she held between her hands rather than a piece of lined A4 when Eddie interrupted her.

'There's a car here for you, Cherry,' he said. He looked excited. 'The driver said that it's something to do with that story you've been chasing all week. He said that his boss told him to tell you that if you go with him now, all will be revealed. Does this make sense to you? Am I going to get my orgy pictures at last?'

Cherry looked up at him incomprehendingly. 'He said what?'

'He said that all will be revealed. You've got to go and find out what he's on about. Do you want me to send Steve after you? Just in case?'

She looked down into the street outside the office and saw that Eddie was right. There was the familiar car. The driver leaned casually against the bonnet while he smoked a cigarette. That bastard Eros.

Cherry weighed up her options. She could refuse to go. But Eddie was right behind her, looking out at the car as if it might give him a clue as to what she had been working on. She could just get in the car. All would be revealed, the driver's boss had promised. She should at least try to get some pictures of that bloody basement that had started it all. She would show Eros that he hadn't scared her.

Even if he had. Though probably not in the way he expected. Cherry shrugged her coat on and hurried down the stairs towards the car.

Eros had managed to scare Cherry by showing her that she wasn't invulnerable to the power of good sex and plain old animal attraction. He had shown her that she wasn't immune to losing her head over a man.


It was the first time Cherry had arrived at the house in broad daylight. It looked different. Not only because of the daylight; the curtains were open and the house looked lived in again. It didn't seem possible that so much had happened in the lobby she now walked through. There was no sign that, on the night of the orgy, naked buttocks had slid down the banisters, or an ex-cabinet minister had given a policeman a blow-job by the double doors that now opened on to a sun-flooded room.

Eros kept her waiting. The driver had told her that

she should stay in the hallway until his master called for her. It was just another way of asserting his superiority, Cherry thought.

When he finally summoned her into his office, Eros sat at his desk at the far end of the room, with a window behind him. Cherry couldn't see his face, just a silhouette. When she shaded her eyes to get a better view she saw that on the desk before him, the golden mask that had fooled her so well stood on a little pedestal looking like a TV award. She felt her stomach lurch at the thought of the first time she had seen the mask. And the first time she had seen the face beneath it.

But that must have been what he was hoping for, of course. He wanted to put her off-guard by reminding her what had happened. She took a deep breath and approached the desk.

'Sit down,' he said.

'I think I'd prefer to stand,' she told him. Somehow, looking down on Eros made her feel more prepared to fight him. Now that she drew closer, she could also see that his perfect face had been somewhat marred since their last meeting. A white cotton-wool pad was strapped to his nose with surgical tape. Clearly the results of the punch she had thrown so expertly.

'Had a nose job?' she asked him cruelly.

'Perhaps I should have taken the opportunity to get a few other things fixed at the same time,' Eros almost laughed. 'But thank you for enquiring. It isn't broken. Only bruised.'

'I'll try harder next time,' she told him. 'What do you want, Eros?'

'My driver was supposed to have told you. I want to reveal all.'

'This isn't one of your shows,' she snorted.

'Isn't it?' He rose from his seat and walked around his desk so that it was no longer between them. 'I did this all for you, Cherry. I wanted this to be your own, special show.'

Cherry made a pretence at clutching her sides to stop them from splitting with laughter. 'My own special show?' she mocked.

'I wanted you to have some magic in your life,' he continued, his mouth twisting ever so slightly into a smile. 'You always seem so bitter when you write your column.'

'Well, thank you,' she smiled. 'But you really needn't have bothered.'

'I wanted you to take me seriously,' he said, and this time his face looked serious too. 'When it became clear that I wasn't going to impress you with any old show – erotic as a ham sandwich, wasn't that the phrase? – I tried to devise something special, something that would show you what I have to offer.'

'I saw a great deal of what many people had to offer here,' said Cherry, remembering the genteel party that had descended into an orgy.

'But you only really let yourself go with me.'

He reached out and tried to take hold of her hand, but Cherry moved suddenly and left Eros grasping her wrist in what she could only interpret as a threatening gesture. She shook her hand free.

'Don't touch me,' she warned him. 'I didn't come here so that you could make another pass at me. I only came here to tell you that you'll never hear from me again, and in return, I want you to have the decency to stay away from me.'

'That would be a pity. I had hoped that overnight you might have come to see the funny side of it all.'

'I don't find being duped funny.'

'That much I realise now,' he said, subtly rubbing at his bandaged nose. 'But I wasn't joking when I said that I wished things didn't have to be different between us. I've always been attracted to you, Cherry. Since the first time we met.'

'What? At your first Albert Hall show? You were surrounded by your stable of models.'

'It was long before that.'

Andreas reached into a drawer in his wide polished desk and brought out the little wooden box. He placed it between them.

'Remember this?'

Cherry picked up the box and turned it over. In the darkness of the basement, she hadn't noticed the initials scratched on to the bottom of the box. CV. But not for Cherry Valentine. For Claire Vasey, the plain old magician's assistant.

'Where did you get this?'

'You gave it to me. On the beach, beneath the pier. You were just about to go to university. I was just about to take over your job. You promised that you'd come back and see the show when you had time. I don't think you ever did.'

Cherry shook her head. As she stared at Eros in disbelief, a long forgotten memory began to reform. The pier. The beach. The black-haired boy that Lorenzo had chosen as his new assistant. Cherry had shown the new boy how to set up Lorenzo's equipment. Then the boy had shown her how to perform a few more useful tricks.

'I think I fell in love with you that night. I looked out for you every weekend. Every time I thought you might be home from college for a while I was on tenterhooks, waiting for you to show up. After three years I gave up, but then we met again. At the after-show party for my first London show. I knew it was you straightaway, but it was clear that you didn't know me.'

'It's been ten years. I'm sure you've changed.'

'So have you. I couldn't believe that the girl I met on the pier had turned into such a hard-nosed hack. You'd even changed your name.'

'And you haven't?'

'I needed to,' he told her. 'Cherry, I never understood why you were so cruel about my work.'

'I was cruel about your work because I didn't enjoy it. I didn't owe you a good review because we met once upon a time,' she told him flatly, placing the box back on the table to underline her resolve.

'We did more than "meet". And you enjoyed yourself here, didn't you? That was my work, Cherry. I brought everyone here for you. I created the illusion. I made the boy turn into a leopard. I painted the frescos that you spent so long admiring. I spiked Eddie's "quit smoking" tape so that he would instruct you to come here. I even dressed up as a chauffeur and drove the bloody car.'

'That was you?'

'Of course it was. But I was also the man in the golden mask. You were ready to fall in love with me, Cherry. You told me so, yourself.'

He reached out for her hand again and this time she didn't move away quickly enough. He raised her fingers to his lips and kissed them, and Cherry, despite herself, found herself closing her eyes languorously at his touch.

'I'm not falling for this,' she told herself out loud. 'You make a habit of this, don't you? Seducing women with the same tricks you use on an audience. Making them think that just because you can pull a rabbit out of a hat that you can have some kind of control over other human beings. Well, we're not in the bloody dark ages now.'

She pulled her hand away again.

'You're the one who has taken control of me,' he said, almost plaintively.

'My God. Tell me you didn't hypnotise me as well?' she said suddenly. 'That tape in the car? It was then, wasn't it? You hypnotised me, too. No wonder I had such weird dreams. I should sue you. I will bloody sue you. And Eddie will too when I tell him what you've done. You'll be finished,' she spat.

'But I couldn't have made you do anything you didn't want to do, Cherry,' Andreas pleaded. 'You told me that yourself once upon a time.'

The genuinely anxious tone of his voice almost softened her.

'Don't you remember? You told me to look deep into your eyes and concentrate on your voice while you counted me to sleep. You told me that you were going to make me fall in love with you but you said it would only work if I really wanted it too.'

Cherry opened her mouth to say something sharp

in reply but couldn't. Though she couldn't remember the first time they met very clearly, she knew that Eros was probably telling the truth. The hypnotism trick. Eighteen and full of the confidence that working in an end of pier show had given her, Cherry had told lots of boys that she could put them under her spell and plenty of them had fallen for it. Or pretended to. 'I can't make you do anything you don't *really* want to do,' she would tell them as she seduced them in the shade of the promenade. When she cruelly dumped them days or weeks later, they would claim that she had ensnared their hearts unfairly. She had been happy to tell herself that her hypnotic powers were an illusion then. No harm done. No hearts really broken. She couldn't put anyone into a trance. Bearing that in mind, she told herself, surely the only way to deal with Eros was to laugh off the way he had tried to dupe her with one of her own old lines.

But Cherry looked at him standing in front of her, his nose all patched up and his eyes as big as saucers behind the bandages, and suddenly she couldn't find a single cutting word. He didn't look much like a sex god now. But she had to admit that there was still something about him. When he held her hand and kissed it, she had been flooded with warmth at his touch, just as she had been that first time in the bedroom before she knew who he was. When his eyes drifted slowly down her body, mentally divesting her of her clinging jersey dress as they went, she didn't feel entirely affronted. She felt as though ghostly fingers were wrapping themselves around her buttons and popping them open. When he looked at her face, she could feel his soft lips on her cheek.

Eros sighed and looked away from her to the little box he had kept for almost fifteen years. He sat in his high-backed leather chair and crossed his feet on the desk.

'It's not going to happen, is it?' he said to her. 'You can't see beyond the picture of me that you've drawn for yourself. You can't reconcile the man who held you last night with the man you see in front of you now. You refuse to believe that these hands can touch you again like they did last night, and won't allow yourself to discover whether it was the man or the strangeness of the situation that captivated you then. You prefer to think that you were tricked, that when I touched you like I did, when I stroked your neck and told you that you were beautiful, you prefer to think that I was lying. You prefer to think that it was only I who got any pleasure out of being with you that night, and that most of that pleasure was to do with revenge for a few crappy reviews. You want to deny that you were moved by me, that you called out to heaven and begged that the moment would never end.'

He looked at her steadily all the while he was saying this, and much as Cherry wanted to block his words out, she found that she couldn't. For a moment, she was paralysed in his gaze. Then she saw the corner of his mouth twitch upwards and they both burst out laughing. They were back beneath the pier again. Only just adult. Playing at love. The sunshine flooded through the tall windows of the office and for a moment it was that summer so many years ago.

'What's so funny?' he said when they'd managed to stop.

It was Cherry's turn to pull a serious face now. 'I think I've just had my lightbulb moment,' she said.

'Is that a good thing?'

She nodded. 'It's a very good thing.'

She let her eyes roam over his face with a new outlook. How ridiculous to have felt so bitter. She hadn't noticed how kind his smile was before. She hadn't noticed that he had a sense of humour when he wasn't acting up on stage. She hadn't noticed that there really was no reason why they shouldn't be together again.

'There's only one more thing I have to know before I can really trust you,' she said. 'I can't remember your real name.'

'Andrew,' he said. 'Andrew Smith.'

Cherry smiled at the floor.

'What's funny about that?' he asked.

She was remembering her day of sleuthing in the paper's library. Mr Smith. So that *wasn't* a made-up name.

'Andrew suits you much better,' she told him. 'I think that was half the problem with you. I just couldn't bring myself to believe that I could love someone called Andreas. But Andrew? I like that.'

Andrew smiled with relief as Cherry wrapped her arms around his neck.

'But you know, there are a couple of other things that you might have to change about yourself too, before we can really start again.'

'Anything,' he whispered, planting a kiss in her flower-scented hair.

'Well,' she whispered. 'You've got to lose this shirt.'

She unbuttoned the white silk shirt and pushed it off his shoulders. 'And this belt. Far too fancy.' She pulled the belt from its loops and let it join the shirt on the floor. 'And I can't possibly take you seriously while you're still wearing these leather trousers.'

Andrew practically purred with delight as he heard the sound of his zipper being tugged down.

'And would that make me your perfect man?' he asked her.

She inched the tight trousers down over his hips. He covered her hands with his own and helped her to get them down as far as his ankles.

'Almost perfect,' Cherry assured him. She slipped her hands inside his silky underpants and cupped his firm square buttocks.

Their lips touched again. There was no anger now, just affection. Delicately. Cherry took Andrew's plump lower lip between her teeth and bit him gently. When she released him, he plunged his tongue into her mouth.

Stepping out of his leather trousers for what would be the last time, Andrew wrapped his arms around Cherry and held her tight against him. Pressing her hand against his chest as they kissed, she fancied that she could feel his heart beating beneath her fingers. His pulse in tune with her pulse. She let her hand slip lower, stroking lovingly over his belly, pausing momentarily at the waistband of his pants, before she slipped her hands inside them again and this time paid attention to his pulsing shaft.

Meanwhile, his hands wandered all over her body, fast and frantic as though he thought she might change her mind. But there was no danger of that. Cherry knew what she wanted now. She wanted him. She wanted his mouth on hers. She wanted his shaft inside her as they made love.

Soon they were rolling on the expensive Persian carpet in front of Andrew's desk. Cherry was giggling as he pulled her dress up over her head. His hot breath on her stomach as he kissed around her belly button made her shiver happily. She twisted his thick black hair in her hands and rolled her head from side to side as his tongue sent her into ticklish ecstasies.

When he put his hand between her legs, he found her already wet and ready. She wrapped her legs around his back playfully. With her hand on the back of his head, she drew his mouth down on hers for a kiss.

'You still haven't explained what a lightbulb moment is,' he murmured, his mouth so close to hers that she could feel his lips moving against her lips.

'It's when you realise that resistance is useless,' she told him. 'It's when you realise that you might have found the one.'

Their joined lips smiled.

Cherry tilted her pelvis so that Andrew's penis couldn't help but push its way inside her. She grasped his buttocks to pull him further in, until they were absolutely joined again, smiling into one another's eyes with the delighted realisation that this was what they both wanted.

Cherry threw back her head in ecstasy as they began to move. She knew that she wouldn't be able to last long this time. She wanted to explode with joy. It was as though the foreplay for this meeting had been going on for years. Andrew groaned softly as he ground his body against hers. Cherry clutched at the back of his head, holding him against her. She filled her lungs with the warm scent of his body and the intoxicating swirl of arousal that enveloped their bodies like smoke.

'I love you,' he told her again. 'I love you, I love you, I love you.' A protestation for each time he thrust into her.

Cherry arched her body up from the carpet to be closer to him. She didn't want their bodies to be disconnected for even a second. As he withdrew his shaft, she pressed herself against him, willing him back inside her. Willing him to come.

Their orgasms arrived like the crashing of a bow wave on a lighthouse rock. They roared simultaneously and held hard to each other's bodies. Cherry felt the repercussions through every nerve in her body. It was as though, until this moment, she had never fully been alive.

Andrew felt it too. He let himself be totally engulfed by the wave of passion that overpowered him. Lying there together, coming together, on the floor of that room, they were finally stripped of all illusions. The pumping of their bodies was utterly true. Utterly real.

Panting on the carpet when her orgasm was over and Andrew had pulled away to recover himself, Cherry gazed up at the ceiling. With the sun creeping in through the window to caress their bodies, she knew that the moment was perfect. She reached out her hand to touch Andrew's arm. He turned towards her and smiled.

'What's funny?' she asked, when the smile turned to another laugh.

'Go on,' he said. 'You can admit it now.'

'OK, Andreas,' Cherry sighed. 'You were magic.'